STONE ARMY

A Stone Cold Thriller

J. D. WESTON

FREEDOM

HEADLIGHTS SHONE LIKE TWO DYING SUNS AT THE FAR reach of Gabriella's vision, growing closer, burning brighter, and blinding her watering eyes. It was as if a searing needle had penetrated her visual organs and found the sensitive nerves cowering behind. Beneath her feet, the ground rumbled, silent but growing in intensity like the rising chaos of a stampede.

She turned to face the sound of breaking branches, barking dogs and men's voices, which had raised to a fever pitch. In the darkness of the forest, Gabriella saw torch beams cutting the night, leaving no escape except onwards across the railway tracks and into the unknown.

A distant scream pierced the blackness somewhere far away. The barking of dogs changed from the howl of an excited hunting pack to snappy snarls as they cornered their prey and pinned it to the ground.

"Donna," whispered Gabriella.

A faint cloud formed when she spoke as the night air met her warm breath.

Another scream sounded followed by frantic struggles as,

somewhere in the darkness, her friend fought off the dogs. A dark image formed in Gabriella's mind of the German Shepherds she had seen prowling the fence line of the laboratory. She saw an image of the pack, excited by the hunt as they tore at Donna's clothes, their teeth clamping down on her hands and arms, pulling her to the ground, their ferocity far outweighing that of the men who followed her with torchlights.

In front of Gabriella, two sets of railway tracks ran left to right from the coast to the mainland. Beyond the tracks, the ground fell away to fields and a forest columned by the night; dark outlines against a dark sky. Somehow, after her ordeal, the black unknown beyond seemed calm and safe in comparison to what lay behind. But something made her stand still. To cross the train lines and escape into the darkness would mean failure. But returning to the hunting dogs and torchlight men would mean certain death.

Some voices called out to others that they'd found one. Gabriella hesitated, undecided. A single gunshot into the air, followed by the lighting of a flare, marked the spot. The searching torches turned and headed that way, bouncing through the dark forest. The flash of the muzzle and burning flare found its way to Gabriella's watering eyes, registering enough danger to trigger the carnal instincts to run and find help. But a stronger fear of failure glued her to the spot.

"We got one," called a voice. "Find the other one. She went that way. She can't be far."

That voice. The voice that taunted Gabriella's drug-fuelled dreams and darkened her miserable days.

A torchlight span in a wide arc close by. It shone through the trees, tracing Gabriella's path through the long grass and up onto the embankment where she stood, frozen to the spot. The vibration beneath her feet was accompanied by the grumble of an approaching train.

The heavy pounding in Gabriella's chest amplified the sound of her breathing. She could feel the drug working. Whatever it was, it fuelled the familiar rush of blood to her head, the invincible surge of energy that coursed through her body, and the trembling of what felt like every muscle in her body, holding her taut like a runner on the starting blocks.

A man broke through the trees. His beam of light cut the darkness like a long, straight snake. The dark form was unmistakable. Broad square shoulders. His head cocked to one side. The swagger of a man who feared nothing.

That man.

He was different to the others. He was cruel, with a voice that violated Gabriella and the girls, and with eyes that did more than undress her; they seemed to tear at her clothes just like the dogs tearing at Donna.

His torchlight found Gabriella. It blinded her and fixed her to the spot. There was no need for words; she could sense his leering grin behind the light.

In the distance, the dogs silenced, and a group of torch-lights flashed in all directions as they began their hunt for Gabriella. The dark man in front of her glanced back as if he was considering calling out. But he changed his mind and returned his attention to his quarry.

His prize.

Gabriella took one step back. Her bare foot found the track, cold and hard, but buzzing with energy like the muscles in her body that tensed and relaxed with adrenaline.

Gabriella held his stare. The man responded with a look, daring her with silent taunts to run and inviting her to him with unheard charm. He gave a flick of his eyes to the distant oncoming train. She saw his delight in the sight of her last remaining seconds on earth, half-naked, scared and broken.

"It seems to me that you have three choices," he said.

An agonised scream came from the woods behind him.

But it wasn't a scream as Gabriella understood the word. It was more of the final, anguished wail of a tortured, dying girl, and a submission to death.

"Three choices?" said Gabriella.

She shunned the sound of her friend's death from her mind, seeking solace in the growing rumble beneath her foot.

"First choice," said the man, "you can run. You can cross those tracks and run like you've got the devil on your heels and he's mad as hell at you. But you won't get far. I know those fields like I know the skin on my hand. I'll find you before you even break for breath."

The concentrated torchlights in the forest dispersed as each of the men spread out to find Gabriella. A slice of light lit the side of the man's face, revealing a knowing smile that he had her all to himself.

Dogs barked in the trees to her left, where Gabriella had stripped and run through the freezing stream. The men called out, whooping with delight and joking that the last girl was already naked. Removing her clothes was intended to buy Gabriella time and throw the dogs off her scent. But the screams of Donna had stalled her escape.

"Second choice," said the man, "you can come down off the embankment. I'll give you my coat and I'll take you back. No-one will hurt you. I can assure you."

"Just like nobody hurt Donna?" said Gabriella.

But the man responded with a shrug.

Rounding the long bend, the headlights of the oncoming train swept across the trees, then lit one side of Gabriella's body. The rumbling beneath her foot intensified, vibrating through her body, and the sound of the horn broke the night as if marking her two choices. Run or return.

"And what's option three?" she asked between horns, shouting above the noise of the approaching train.

The torchlight flicked off.

In the darkness, only shadows and dark shapes moved. The headlights of the train passed by the tree line, lighting only the grass, the tracks and Gabriella herself, growing wider as the train thundered closer.

Another horn as the driver urged her to move.

The ground shook with a pulse matching Gabriella's heartbeat.

But she stayed.

A backward step would commit to the run, triggering the man and the dogs into action. A forward step would admit defeat. He'd take her into his lying, devilish arms and use her for the evil he'd been dreaming of since that first day. Then he'd kill her.

But staying on the tracks offered her only real chance of escape, to a place where even he couldn't reach her.

But death would mean failure.

Another horn, louder and longer.

The squeal of brakes as two hundred tons of steel anchored, spraying great washes of sparks into the forest.

"Option three," he said, appearing beside her from nowhere.

He smiled the smile she'd seen a thousand times in her dreams, in her waking tortured days, and now, as death held her in its bony grip. The surprise caught her off guard. She stepped back, and stood centrally between the tracks, where he seemed to dare not follow.

With half his face lit by the approaching train, he leaned across to her with an outstretched hand. "Don't be stupid, Gabriella. Come with me."

But Gabriella smiled and closed her eyes, letting peace find her, bringing with it the calm that allowed her to focus on cherished memories. She searched through her life in just a few seconds. An image of her father smiling in his garden as he stopped turning the earth and leaned on his garden fork to admire her, fanning himself with his wide-brimmed hat. Her brother shooting her a wink as he led Gabriella from their home on one of their many adventures. She would sleep in the car. Francis would drive then wake her up when they had reached the destination. Each time it was a different location, carefully planned and designed to enthral young Gabriella. Sometimes it was the beach. Sometimes Francis would park at the top of a hill to look down at the rolling forests below. They would sit and drink coffee from a flask and perhaps eat a croissant.

On one occasion, Francis had taken her to Paris to see the Christmas lights, but the memory was snatched away before she could relive the moment.

"Gabriella," called the man.

Her name came to her as he haunted her last treasured moments on earth. The images of her loved ones faded away, but without regret.

The train horn sounded once more, loud and urgent.

The beat of the tracks moved the ground on which she stood.

And the drug that coursed through her body woke every living cell, firing energy into every single muscle.

"*Gabriella*," said the man, his hand clutching for her arm.

Another loud horn. The headlights, as bright as the sun, held the two of them in limbo. The ground, the trees, the whole world, was white.

His outstretched arm.

Those evil eyes.

Men burst from the forest behind him and stopped as the train bore down on her like a raging beast. She had just one second of life remaining. One second to deny evil its glory. One second to cherish living.

"I die for France," she said.

Then ran.

2

OVER THE HILLS AND FAR AWAY

THIN, WISPY BRANCHES OF WILLOW TORE AT HARVEY'S FACE as he broke new trails on the river bank in the South of France. But even the stinging slices to his face weren't enough to deter him or provoke a stumble. The rhythmic beat of his heart in time with his pace was enough to force him on, pumping harder, striding longer. The faster he ran, the harder his heart thumped.

A fallen tree blocked the path but he hurdled it with ease then ran down to a stream. His foot found the cold water; it splashed up his leg, fresh and cool. Beyond the stream was a long uphill stretch, littered with saplings and thorny bushes. Finding his way through without breaking stride was tough, and his legs took the brunt of the attack. Sharp pointed thorns dug into his skin and carved deep cuts across his legs. But with his arms pumping, and his mind fixed on reaching the top, he forced himself forwards, pushing the pain aside and focusing on one step after the other.

At the top of the hill, a narrow path led through the trees. It was a regular route for dog walkers who had trodden the path to a flatbed of dry mud. Even the trees had allowed a route through them. With every ounce of energy left in his legs, Harvey ploughed on. His downhill strides increased in length as gravity took hold. Then he broke through the tree line at the foot of the hill and entered a wide open field dominated by long grass and wildflowers.

The gate at the end of the field was just a dot. It was a goal to reach like so many other gates in Harvey's life. A place or a time where he passed from one field to the next. One battle to another. One life to more life.

The dog walkers' pathway circumvented the wild grass at the edge of the field, beside raspberry and blackberry bushes and dotted with rabbit holes. But Harvey stormed ahead, as he'd always done, forging his own way through the field, through the battles, and through life.

A glimpse of sun marked the end of the morning twilight. It was Harvey's favourite time, when enough light spilled across the earth to see the day after the night. But few did see it every morning.

For the last three hundred metres, Harvey gave everything he had. He searched deep for some pocket of power that his body had stored, some piece of mental strength that he needed now, to push harder than before.

Harvey slammed into the gate at full speed, using the flex of the wood to absorb his momentum. Then, with his hands raised behind his head, he stretched while gaining control of his pulse. A single bead of sweat ran down his face, hung from his chin, and then fell away as he lowered himself to his knees. The thunder of his heart in his ears eased to reveal a new sound, foreign to the early morning. The nearby thump of twin rotor blades grew closer as his body quietened. In the sky to his right, above the raised railway embankment, a helicopter hovered against the dawning sky with a bright spotlight washing from side to side and heading his way.

Dogs barked and deep voices called out, anxious and angry, like the voices of military men.

The five-hundred-yard walk back to his small house was Harvey's warm down. In his younger years, he would have run the entire way. But with each passing year, the warm down seemed to be getting longer. Harvey didn't mind. The time gave him thinking space. But the circling chopper was growing closer with each step. Whatever the police were looking for, Harvey wanted nothing to do with it. There were only three hundred yards to the main road, where Harvey could cross the small country lane and head into the fields to his small farmhouse by the beach, where a log fire would warm him and the views of the Mediterranean would occupy his mind.

He ducked beneath a copse of trees as the helicopter made a pass. The noise was deafening in the early morning silence. But it faded as the helicopter circled back towards the railway, giving Harvey a window to escape to the forest and into the fields behind his house, leaving whatever was happening behind him.

The roof of his house was visible through the trees and beyond the road. A thin wisp of smoke from the chimney, barely visible in the half-light, let Harvey know that the logs in his fireplace would need replacing.

Approaching the road, with just a wide ditch to hurdle, Harvey sprinted to make the jump, launching from his right foot and stretching out with his left leg.

But something stopped him mid-jump.

Two hands reached up and caught his foot then dragged him to the ground, where he slammed gut-first into the far side of the ditch. He rolled in time to see a girl throw herself at him. Her contorted face was a mix of anger and terror, and her muddied fingers were outstretched, ready to rip at his throat.

Harvey rolled to one side, avoiding the wild girl's hands, then doubled back to pin her down. She landed with his leg across her back and his hand on her neck, forcing her face into the mud.

"Let me go," she begged, her voice muffled by the long grass. "Please. Let me go."

"Who are you?" said Harvey.

But the girl hesitated.

Harvey pushed harder.

In the distance, the thumps of the helicopter's rotors grew louder.

"Are they looking for you?" said Harvey.

Again, the girl failed to respond.

But as the helicopter grew closer, with surprising strength and agility, and in one smooth move, the girl twisted from Harvey's grip until they were face to face. She then slipped beneath him, like a slippery eel, and dropped back into the ditch.

Harvey spun around to find her pulling the long grass over herself and sitting with her back against the wall of the ditch. The helicopter slowed then dropped to a hover, sending loose grass and debris scattering across the field.

Harvey climbed to his feet as the chopper came down, then brushed the mud from his legs, catching the girl's wide, fearful eyes as he did.

A silent plea for Harvey's silence.

The helicopter doors opened on both sides.

Harvey glanced at the girl.

"Please help me," she mouthed.

"Find her," screamed Cassius Kane, before sweeping the contents of his walnut-wood desk onto the floor.

"We're trying, sir," said Jones.

"Someone is going to pay for this," said Kane. He kicked his desk telephone across the room and stepped out from the mess. Then he turned and raised a single index finger at Jones. "I've got one dead girl who looks as if she's been eaten by dogs and one missing girl who knows enough to have us put away for life. Everything the law would need to lock us up for good is in that girl's head and running through her veins."

"I'm aware-"

"Don't stand there and tell me what you're aware of. What are you doing here anyway? The last time I looked, she was out there somewhere, not in here."

"We're searching the area," said Jones. "It's like she vanished into thin air."

"If you don't find her, Jones, it's game over for all of us. You, me, and every single one of your men."

"We'll find her, sir."

"This isn't the military now, Jones. We don't have the luxury of the government on our side. We crossed that line a long time ago. All she has to do is point us out."

"I'm aware of who we are, sir, and what we've done. And so are the men."

"Exactly how far are you willing to go?" said Kane. "And your men? How many of them would die for the cause?"

"Every single one of them. I can vouch for them."

"We're riding a thin line. If we succeed, we'll have a future. But if we fail, it's game over for all of us. We're talking life in prison here, Jones. No parole. No visitors. We'd all vanish like farts in the wind. We wouldn't even get an extra pillow if we asked for it. Do you understand the gravity of the situation?"

"I understand, sir. I remember the deal," replied Jones. The vein on his temple stood proud and blue as he cocked his head to one side. "You fund the project. We keep it secure."

"And have I funded the project, Jones?"

"Yes, sir."

"And have you kept it secure?"

Jones sucked at his top lip, which accentuated his lean features.

"No," said Kane. "No, you haven't."

"It would help if we had a few more details, sir," said Jones, meeting Kane's stare.

"Details?"

"What are we up against here?" said Jones. "We found two of our men with their throats torn out this morning."

Kane's eye twitched at the news.

"And it wasn't dogs, sir," said Jones.

"It's just a girl, Jones," said Kane, planting his hands behind his back and pacing the length of the room.

"Sir, we need to know the truth. We know it's some kind of drug. If it was *just* a girl, two of my men would still be alive."

"Do you have any idea at all where she went?" asked Kane, ignoring Jones' whining and performing a relaxed turn to set his pacing off in the other direction.

"All we have is a pile of her clothes. The smart little bitch tore them off to throw the dogs off her scent," said Jones.

Kane stepped across to the window. His silver hair appeared almost blonde in the reflection, but the lines beneath his eyes were clear as the daylight now hovering over the horizon, where in the distance, the town of Saint-Pierre sat peacefully beside the calm waters of the Mediterranean.

"I want her alive, Jones," said Kane. He felt his eye twitch once more. "I've worked too hard to clear our names. I won't let this little French tart ruin it for us."

"It's freezing out there. No-one could survive the night without clothes. If we do find her, there's a good chance she'll be dead already."

"You don't know who we're dealing with here," said Kane.

"It's just a girl, you said."

"It's a girl alright. It was you who kidnapped her. I just enhanced her," said Kane. He smiled at Jones in the window. "Doctor Farrow has been pumping her full of chemicals for a month. She's high as a kite, charged like a battery and, by all accounts, doesn't die easily."

"Pumped her full of what?" said Jones. "What is she capable of? She tore the throats out of our team, sir, two fully grown men twice her weight and size."

"She's just getting started," said Kane. "But she'll hit withdrawal soon and come begging for more."

"Just getting started, sir? We only have fifteen men. We're down to thirteen and the prime minister arrives in two days' time. If I'm sending men to get her, I want to know what she can and cannot do. Know your enemy, sir. The first rule of war. You taught me that."

"She's not superhuman, Jones. This isn't some miracle drug that Doctor Farrow has been concocting like some mad evil genius." Kane paused to ensure he had Jones' full attention. "But it is close."

Jones cocked his head to one side, a trait that annoyed Kane.

"Do you work out, Jones?"

"Yes, of course," he replied, with a subconscious glance at his body.

"How far can you run?"

"Before failing?"

"Yes," said Kane. "How far can you run before your legs collapse and your insides feel as if they're hanging by threads?"

"I've done a marathon, sir. I did it a couple of years ago," said Jones. "Aside from that, the army made me run every day."

"But to do that marathon, you had to pace yourself, right? You didn't just run flat out for twenty-six miles, did you? And even the army doesn't make you sprint until you collapse."

"No, of course not."

Kane nodded. "You lift weights?"

"Yes, sir," said Jones, with another glance at his arms. "I stay in shape. You know I do."

"And what happens when you hit the end of a session? You can barely lift your own arms, right? Your legs feel like jelly and your body screams for protein to repair the damage you've done."

"That's an accurate assessment, sir."

Kane nodded. "Chess," he said.

"Chess, sir?"

"Do you play?" said Kane.

"I've never really been one for board games, sir."

"Do you read, at least?" said Kane, unsurprised at the lack of intellect displayed by his second in command.

"Yes, sir. I read."

"And what do you read? Please tell me it's not the Beano."

"No. Books, sir. I like books."

"Good. What was the last book you read?"

"I don't know," said Jones, cocking his head once more and staring at the ceiling as he tried to remember the name of a book.

"Okay. Okay. Enough of the mental challenges, Jones." Kane pushed off the window sill and stepped back to his desk. He picked up his phone and scattered papers, then began to arrange them into a neat pile. "What if I told you that Doctor Farrow's creation could make you run a marathon flat out? No stopping."

"Sprinting?"

"Sprinting, Jones, from start to finish. And those training sessions when your legs feel like jelly and you can barely lift your arms? You could go for another hour at least."

"Respectfully, sir, that's not possible."

"Au contraire, Jonesy. You see, the drug is split into two separate chemicals. The first one, when taken individually, can push your body to the maximum. It finds those resources your body stores away, and when those are depleted, it'll eat away at things the body doesn't need and transform them into energy."

"Like what?"

"Like fat, Jones. Like tumours. Even muscle if you push hard enough. It becomes a living thing inside you, stealing resources from anything that uses your body's energy. If you push too hard, it'll start using the body's organs. That's what Farrow was testing."

"That's why three of the girls died?" asked Jones, his voice hushed as if they could be overheard and were disclosing secrets.

Kane nodded and glanced at him before lowering his eyes and steepling his fingers.

"They were on an early formula. Farrow has perfected it now."

"What about the second chemical?"

Pleased to move on, Kane looked back up at Jones. "What happens when you push too hard? If you're running and your body can't keep up?"

"I slow down."

"Why do you slow down?"

"I don't know. I guess my brain tells me to."

"What if that line of communication was blocked?" said Kane. "What if there was a drug that could push you harder than ever before and your brain was unable to receive messages telling it to stop? What if the harder you pushed, the greater the effect? The harder you'd run, the more energy you'd have. The more weights you'd lift, the easier it would become to lift more."

"I'd be superhuman."

"Not quite, Jones," said Kane. "But you'd be damn near unstoppable. You'd be in a self-fulfilling state. It's called SFS."

"Why did you ask about the reading?" said Jones. "I don't get what that has to do with it."

"Okay. Imagine this. You're pumped full of SFS. You've entered a state where every muscle in your body is running at full whack. It's not just your body that is heightened, your brain is a muscle too. You'd remember everything you've ever read, heard, seen, and smelled. Even the finest detail could be recalled."

"So we're talking about people with self-fulfilling states of energy essentially fuelling themselves, with no switch to turn them off, and who can remember the smallest detail. And we made that here?"

"Exactly," said Kane, leaning back in his chair and allowing himself a smile, despite the circumstances. "You're imagining what it would be like, aren't you? You're imagining how big those arms of yours would be. How fast you could run. How smart you'd become."

"It's hard not to imagine the possibilities," said Jones, running his hand across his shaved head, embarrassed by his selfish imagination.

"That's where you and I differ, Jones," said Kane. "While you are picturing how many girls you'd get and how they'd admire your body and possibly even your brain…" He leaned forwards onto his desk, linked his fingers and fixed Jones in his stare. "I'm imagining an army."

3

GALLOWS POLE

TWO MEN ARMED WITH AUTOMATIC WEAPONS DROPPED TO the ground. Gabriella peered through the grass, her eyes flicking between the helicopter and the man she had thought was one of them. They took up defensive positions, scouring the field. A man wearing all black stepped down. His face was concealed by the grass but Gabriella recognised him, the way he stood with his back ramrod straight, as if he'd spent his entire life on military parade. He ducked low until he'd cleared the still-turning blades. Then he strode towards the jogger, who met him halfway to avoid drawing attention to Gabriella's hiding place.

Anxiety triggered a pulse of adrenaline through her body. She searched for an exit but saw only the road and more fields.

She wouldn't stand a chance.

The man in black showed the jogger a printed picture of Gabriella, gesticulating the direction from which she had run. The jogger seemed to remain calm with his arms folded across his chest. He appeared unfazed by the armed men who surrounded the chopper. The interaction seemed to take an age. Jones was asking questions, probably trying to trip up the jogger. But he responded only with shakes of his head.

Following the conversation was simple.

The man in black asked the jogger if he was sure he hadn't seen Gabriella.

The jogger confirmed with a shake of his head, while the man in black described Gabriella, holding his hand up at her approximated five-foot-six height.

The jogger shook his head.

The last question asked the jogger why he was covered in mud, with a gesture to his knees and running shirt.

From where Gabriella was hidden, the jogger appeared not to answer, only offering a shrug response and closing off the conversation.

The questioning finished with the man in black offering the jogger a card with a number to call if he saw someone of Gabriella's description. The jogger pocketed it without looking at the printed details then nodded, and the man in black signalled to both the pilot and the guards to wind it up and enter the helicopter.

Even when the doors had closed, and the rotor began to pick up speed, the jogger remained standing between the chopper and Gabriella's hiding place as if he was protecting her. He shielded his eyes, waiting for them to leave. Only when the helicopter had ascended, banked, and was well into its flight did the jogger turn and walk back to Gabriella. She stared at him with a mixed look of gratitude and uncertainty.

He stopped a few feet from the ditch, returning Gabriella's stare until she broke away. There was something in his eyes. A confidence. A history. A fearlessness.

"Who were those men?" he asked, removing his sweater.

"If I told you, you wouldn't believe me."

He tossed Gabriella the sweater and waited for her to pull it on before looking back. She tugged it down to her legs as far as it would stretch then gave him a grateful half-smile. Gabriella stood, but she said nothing.

The man pointed towards the beach road.

"If you go that way, you'll hit a town. It's about an hour's walk. Keep to the tree line and stay out of sight. You can keep the sweater," he said, then turned to leave.

"Wait," said Gabriella.

The jogger stopped but didn't turn. He took a deep breath as if he was aggravated. As Gabriella climbed from the ditch, the man remained facing the other way, defiant, as if nothing was going to change his mind.

"Aren't you going to ask why they're after me?"

"None of my business," he replied. "If you're mixed up in something, that's your business."

"They kidnapped me. I escaped. I don't know who they are. That's the truth."

"The men with the helicopter and armed security kidnapped you?"

"That's right."

"And you don't know who they are?"

"No."

"How long ago did they take you?"

"I'm not sure. A month maybe. They killed my friends," said Gabriella. She felt the tail-end of her sentence waver as the thought of Donna and the sound of her dying screams filled her mind. "They set dogs on us."

"Where?" he asked.

"I don't know. I've been running all night. I don't even know which direction. From Saint-Pierre, I think. But I can't be sure."

"Saint-Pierre is twenty miles away."

"I ran all night."

With visible reluctance, the jogger turned, giving Gabriella time to take in his strong features: a short crop of dark hair atop a lean face and piercing eyes. But she couldn't make out the colour.

"So who are you?" He asked the question like it was a duty he could do without.

"I'm Gabriella."

The jogger didn't reply.

"Gabriella DuBois," she said, hoping her full name might invoke some kind of response, some indication he would help her.

He looked as if he was going to respond, but instead, for the first time, he looked her up and down, sizing her up, until the stare became uncomfortable. Gabriella pulled the sweater down below her underwear.

"Two women are kidnapped. They escape. The captors set dogs on them, killing one. But the other one, somehow, manages to escape and run through the night, half naked. A private helicopter is sent out with an armed detail to find her?"

"That's right," said Gabriella.

"Then you're hiding something," said the man. "Kidnappers don't usually have helicopters at their disposal. Nor do they have an armed security unit."

"You have experience in such matters?"

The jogger didn't reply.

"You'll help me?" asked Gabriella.

Something in his voice had inferred that he might.

He looked back at the helicopter far off on the horizon and heard the series of barking dogs in the distance.

"No." His voice was void of both emotion and empathy. "I can't be involved."

"Just help me get somewhere safe until dark," she pleaded. "Then I'll move on. Please."

The man didn't reply.

"Please," said Gabriella. "If I stay out here, they'll find me. Do you hear those dogs? They have found my trail. I know they have."

The man didn't reply. He checked the sky again to make sure the chopper wasn't returning then turned back to her. He was going to say yes. Gabriella could sense it. She bit her lower lip in anticipation.

"The next town is an hour's walk. I'd get moving if I were you."

"Wait," said Gabriella.

The man stopped but said nothing.

"You didn't tell me your name."

He turned to face her.

"It's Harvey," he said. "Harvey Stone."

Steaming hot water rained down from the shower, filling the small bathroom with steam. Leaning on the wall with both hands, Harvey closed his eyes and let his head hang low, allowing the water to run across his skin.

The farmhouse he'd bought several years previously was his only possession, save for his beloved motorcycle. It was quiet, clean and simple, and exactly what he needed to escape the convolutions of his criminal past. Surrounded by his own few acres of land and the adjoining forests, it was a small pocket of peace where he could live out his retirement. The simple lifestyle required manual labour as he had to maintain the building. A cord of wood was stacked on one side of the house and his days were spent repairing the roof, painting the windows and tending the small plot of land.

There was no television in the house and no radio, only his laptop and his mobile phone, which was ringing when he emerged from the bathroom wrapping a towel around his waist.

"Melody?" he answered.

"Hey, big man. How's France?" said Melody, unable to disguise her smile even over the phone.

"Quiet."

"Just the way you like it then?"

"Something like that," said Harvey. "How's London?"

"Cold and damp. Everyone's getting ready for Christmas. You should see Oxford Street this year. They've done a great job with the decorations."

"Sounds nice."

Harvey stepped over to the kitchen door and peered out at his small plot of land, making a mental note that he'd need to cover the small vegetable plot that Melody had started during the summer. In the reflection of the glass, his house seemed to have translucent trees across the walls, and the glow of the log burner shone like an orange window in the centre of his land.

"Are you sure you don't want to come and spend Christmas here with Reg, Jess and me?" asked Melody. "I could do with someone to keep me warm."

"We spoke about this already, Melody," replied Harvey. "I'm better here. Besides, I'm not really a Christmas type of guy, am I?"

"Oh, I don't know. I could imagine you dressed up in a little Santa hat. Maybe some tinsel?"

"You know I can't. I'm better off here alone. Things happen whenever I go back to London."

"Only because you let them, Harvey."

"Well, however it happens, it happens. I'll stay here and keep the farmhouse going. You enjoy yourself, and when you come back, we can spend some time together. How does that sound?"

"Like a weak excuse for not coming to see your friends for Christmas. You know we invited Tyler too?"

"They will understand. Tell them I'm sorry."

"Really? The famous Harvey Stone is saying sorry?"

"Well," said Harvey, "not sorry. But they'll understand why I can't come to London."

"So what are you going to do on Christmas day?" asked Melody.

"Sit by the fire. Go for a walk. I don't really know. The same as usual, I guess."

"Don't forget to cover the vegetables. It'll be cold down there by now. Have you done it already?"

"It's on my list."

"You have a list now?" said Melody. "What's on it?"

"It's a short list," said Harvey.

"So tell me."

"Cover the vegetables."

"And?"

"Sit by the fire."

"And?"

"Go for a walk."

"Is that it?"

"It's enough to keep me busy," said Harvey. "What's on your list?"

"Shopping. Drinks with Reg and Jess. More shopping. And I might meet up with some old friends."

"So you won't be sitting by the fire?"

"Reg doesn't have a fire."

"And you won't be going for a walk in the forest?"

"It's London, Harvey."

"So I guess you won't be covering the vegetables either then?"

"Only with olive oil before we put them in the oven."

"Doesn't sound so relaxing."

"Is that your sense of humour coming through again?"

Harvey didn't reply.

"You should relax more, Harvey," said Melody. "I'm liking this funny side of Harvey Stone. Will he still be around when I get back?"

"That depends," said Harvey.

"On what?"

"How much time I get in front of the fire," said Harvey, still peering through the window. A light rain had started to fall, leaving wet dots on the small patio. He watched the drops as Melody spoke. The gaps between each dot grew smaller until the entire area was wet and small pools of water formed on the uneven surface.

"Am I keeping you?" said Melody.

"No," said Harvey.

"Well, I should go anyway. Jess is cooking up a roast for tonight. I think she's practising for Christmas day."

"A roast dinner?" said Harvey, imagining the spread. "I'd come just for that."

"So why don't you?" said Melody, sounding hopeful. "What have you been eating?"

"Fish."

"And?"

"Vegetables."

"Are you sure I can't tempt you? All your friends will be here. Are you really going to let them down just because you're afraid to leave the house?"

"I'm not afraid, Melody."

"So come then. You can make it if you leave today."

"Melody, don't push it."

"Why not? I'd like to spend Christmas with you for once as well. I miss you, Harvey. We all do."

Harvey sucked in a long breath, then exhaled and fogged the window.

"So that's it, is it?" said Melody. "You need to snap out of whatever cloud you're on, Harvey, and have a think about the people that care about you. Trust me, you don't have many. So if I were you, I'd be trying to hold on to whatever friends I had."

"It's lucky you're not me then, Melody," said Harvey, stepping across to the small lounge. He held the phone between his shoulder and his cheek, pulled open the glass door of the log burner, and placed four small logs inside.

"So should I call you tonight?" asked Melody. "I don't want to tear you away from your fire."

"Call if you want. I'm sure I can find the time," said Harvey, closing the small glass door and watching the flames take hold of the fresh fuel.

In the reflection of the glass panel, his kitchen appeared to be ablaze behind him. He watched for a moment as the flames grew higher and the logs settled into place.

"I love you, Harvey Stone," said Melody. "I don't want to fight. Not at Christmas."

"I'll talk to you later," said Harvey.

He dropped the phone from his shoulder into his hand then tossed it onto the couch. He stood and stared down at the log burner, feeling the warmth through his towel. Then he took a fire iron from the bucket of brass tools on the brick fireplace. Dropping to a crouch once more, he opened the burner door and buried the tip of the iron deep into the coals. Then, when the tip was hot enough, Harvey closed the door, stood, and turned to face the room.

"You've got three-seconds to show yourself."

The hard soles of Cassius Kane's service shoes clicked against the pristine, painted, screed floor of his purpose-built research and development centre, a U-shaped, brick building in the grounds of a disused factory. Behind him, Jones walked beside Doctor Farrow, a tall, lean man wearing a white lab coat and thick glasses, with a thin layer of hair pulled across his bald head.

"The subjects escaped from observation room three, sir," said Farrow. "It's just here on the right."

Ahead of Kane was a glass door. It was wide open, revealing a room with two gurneys inside and a small trolley containing a tray of syringes and a tray of vials full of proto-type SFS. A thick plastic-coated cushion material covered the far wall and the floor was spongy underfoot, made of self-levelling rubber. To one side was a glass panel that allowed the staff in the adjacent control room to monitor the subjects. The door was six-inches thick with a similar cushioned material on the inside. Inside the frame, a large electro-magnet aligned with a steel plate to keep the door closed. Only those with an access card could swipe entry and exit to and from the room.

"So this is the observation room?" asked Kane.

"Yes," said Farrow. "It's one of three identical rooms."

"And the other rooms?" said Kane, peering along the corridor.

"All the observation rooms are identical, sir," said Farrow. His voice betrayed his attempt to regain Kane's confidence. "Only I and my staff have access cards. I've retracted all other access cards until we can bridge the design flaw."

"The design flaw?" said Jones. "But it was you who designed this entire facility, Doctor Farrow."

A bitter exchange of hatred passed between the two men in the guise of locked stares and tight lips.

"Let's keep it professional, boys," said Kane, as he walked

across the room and peered into the control room. "There's no sign of a forced exit. No damage?"

"Nothing, sir," said Farrow.

"Jones, how would you get out?" said Kane. "If you were trapped in here, how would you make your escape? Maybe you could offer us an insight into the criminal mind?"

Taking the elevated compliment with all the grace of a bulldog, Jones ran his hand along the inside of the door, then did the same with the frame.

"And they had no implements?" said Jones, directing his question to Farrow.

"None at all. What you see is what you get. We like to reduce the distractions until we need them distracted. If we want to see them run, we bring in a treadmill. If we want to measure their strength, we bring in resistance machines. Nothing is left lying around."

"I don't see how they did it," said Jones. "Someone had to open the doors for them. My men don't have access cards."

"It was the night shift, Mr Jones," said Farrow. "There was nobody here to open the doors for them except the duty doctor."

"And can I presume the duty doctor was observing them?" said Kane. "Being as they were in the observation room?"

"Yes. They were being observed. Both subjects received a dose of undiluted SFS several hours earlier and were being monitored for deterioration."

"Deterioration?" said Jones.

"A comedown. Cold turkey. Whatever you want to call it. All subjects using the older prototype, the diluted mixture, without having a way of working the drug out of their system, experienced severe symptoms."

"Such as?" said Kane.

"Cold sweats. Fever. Cramps. Diarrhoea. Some halluci-nated. One girl tried to tear her own eyes out a few weeks ago," said Farrow. "Her heart gave out before she could manage it fully and she died with her eyeballs hanging from her face."

The statement caught the attention of Kane and Jones, who stared at Farrow with incredulity.

"And you gave these two girls an undiluted batch?" said Kane.

"We had reason to believe the dilution was sending mixed messages. You see, you can take the drug, but it'll have no physical effect at all unless you give it stimulation. Otherwise, the drug will work itself out of your body, leaving you with trace elements. That's why they were getting withdrawal symptoms. We need to be able to administer the drug to hosts for everyday use. The vials in the storeroom are diluted; they are just prototypes. They'll do the job but the withdrawals will be heavy and the effects are less potent. If you're looking for long-term use, the undiluted version provides unmatched results."

"How do you stimulate the drug?" asked Jones.

Farrow glanced at Kane, who nodded his approval at disclosing the information.

"Adrenaline," said Farrow with a smile. "Imagine you have a small army of men, highly trained and each and every one of them with this dormant drug inside them. And then something happens. Something forces them into action. The tension rises. Perhaps they're in battle. Perhaps they're performing a robbery of some kind. The adrenaline kicks in, triggering the SFS and the host fires into life. The rest, as they say, is history."

Jones nodded thoughtfully as if he was considering the possibilities.

"But if they were in the observation room, surely somebody was observing them? Where are they now?"

"The morgue, sir," said Farrow.

Both Kane and Jones raised their eyebrows in surprise.

"Doctor Harold Goldsborough," said Farrow. "He was one of my best."

Again both Kane and Jones stared at the doctor with questioning expressions.

"He swallowed his tongue. We found him on the control room floor. He didn't stand a chance."

"Did you just say he swallowed his tongue?" said Kane.

Farrow nodded.

"How does that have anything to do with how the two girls got out of here?" said Jones.

"It doesn't. But it explains why he didn't try to stop them or raise the alarm," said Farrow.

Kane ran his finger across the glass as he began to pace the circumference of the room. He stopped beside the door and nodded at Jones, who followed him, blocking Farrow's exit.

"You say only those with an access card can open this door from the outside," said Kane.

"There're no manual locks or handles," replied Farrow, with a growing suspicion of what was about to happen.

"And the undiluted SFS, would you call it a finished product?"

"I still have some testing to do," said Farrow. "But I'm quietly confident."

"And where is the undiluted SFS, Doctor Farrow? I want to see the finished product."

"We only made three batches," said Farrow. "We gave two to the test subjects."

"Well, one of them is dead and the other is missing," said Kane. "Where's the third batch?"

Farrow averted his eyes from Kane's stare and studied the floor.

"Farrow?" said Kane. "Where's the undiluted SFS?"

"I need some more time. I just need to run some more tests," said Farrow. "To be sure, you understand?"

"Farrow, I'll ask you one more time," said Kane. "Where is the vial of undiluted SFS?"

"She stole it," said Farrow. "It was missing when I found Doctor Goldsborough this morning. But I can make some more. I just need time."

Kane's hands flexed then bunched into fists. He locked his arms behind his back then stepped outside into the corridor, followed by Jones, who blocked the exit and pulled the door closed behind him.

"Where are you going?" said Farrow, seeing what was happening. "I can make more."

But it was too late. Just as Doctor Farrow launched himself at the door, the magnetic lock kicked into place. All they heard was a dull thump masked by three layers of steel and two layers of padded cushioning.

Kane moved to the control room followed by Jones. They could hear everything the doctor was saying through the internal microphones. On the control desk, among sliders, knobs and switches, was a round, green button marked with the letters MIC.

"This one," said Jones, seeing Kane search for the microphone.

Kane pressed the button with his index finger and it illuminated, green beneath his skin.

"The door works well," said Kane. "I should congratulate you on your design."

"This isn't funny, Kane," said Farrow. He slammed his hand against the glass. "You get me out of here. You'll never find her without me."

"Oh, I'll find her," said Kane.

"The tests aren't finished yet," said Farrow. "There's still a lot to do."

"Yes, you're right, Doctor Farrow. But, as you mentioned, we still have tests to run."

"So you need me?" said Farrow. "Let me out and let me finish the job."

"Oh, I'll need you alright, Doctor Farrow," said Kane with a smile.

4

RED HOUSE

CROUCHED IN THE KITCHEN BEHIND THE CENTRE ISLAND, Gabriella prepared to defend herself. A trickle of warmth fed into her bloodstream and she felt her eyes dilate.

From nowhere, an iron poker swung around the corner where she was hiding. Gabriella ducked, rolled and bounced to her feet, swiping a knife from the block on the counter as the poker slammed against the wooden door.

"I told you I can't help you," said Harvey. His earlier nonchalant expression remained but anger was also shining through.

"I've got nowhere to go," said Gabriella. "I just need a place to hide until the sun goes down. That's all I need."

There was a calmness about Harvey Stone that was rare in men. He dropped the fire iron back into the bucket with the fire tools, then he let his head fall back, and rolled his neck as if he enjoyed the release of tension.

"You've got three seconds to get out of my house," said Harvey. "You've had all the help I can give."

"Just a day," said Gabriella. "That's all I need."

"Three," said Harvey, stepping forward, his eyes finding Gabriella's and locking on tight.

"Don't do this," she replied, holding the knife in front of her but backing away to give herself room to fight.

"Two," said Harvey. He took another step, forcing Gabriella to step back out of the kitchen area. Sliding a knife out from the wooden block, he spun it in his hand then extended his arm with the point of the blade aimed at Gabriella's face.

"Last chance to get out alive," said Harvey, collecting a dish towel with his other hand.

Gabriella glanced at the kitchen door and then back to Harvey.

"You wouldn't hurt a girl, would you?"

"If someone breaks into my house and threatens me with a knife, you'd be surprised at the things I would do. Have you finished stalling for time?"

"Just let me stay," said Gabriella, offering him her best sorrowful look and lowering her knife in a gesture of peace.

As quick as a flash, his knife cut through the air before Gabriella's eyes. She leaned back while returning the attack with a lunge to his torso. But Harvey twisted, arching his back, then delivered a left jab to Gabriella's face. The blow stunned her but triggered a fresh release of chemicals.

Three jabs with her blade were blocked, dodged and avoided by Harvey with a control that was, in Gabriella's mind, almost an art. She dropped to one knee to dodge a series of swipes and lunges from Harvey then slammed her knife down towards Harvey's foot. But he was light on his feet, switching stance in time to deliver a knee to her face. Reeling from the blow, Gabriella staggered back. Through her tangled mass of hair, she saw Harvey approaching fast.

She ducked and weaved to avoid two swipes of Harvey's knife, returning with her own, which he caught with the towel. Then he wrapped it around her hand and twisted until she dropped her knife. Somehow, he managed to twist her over his back and launch her across the room.

Landing on her back on a wooden coffee table, which exploded with a crack of splintered wood, Gabriella rolled and got to one knee in time to see his oncoming punch. She leaned back, and felt the rush of air as Harvey's arm swung past and missed her by fractions of an inch. Then, grabbing a handful of his groin, she squeezed as hard as she could through the towel that was wrapped around his waist.

To Gabriella's surprise, he didn't cry out or retreat. He stared down at her, his lips tight as he fought to control the pain. His strong hand found Gabriella's neck, returning the squeeze with an animal-like strength. For a long moment, the two shared a battle of the tightest grip, and no matter how hard Gabriella tried, the tightness on her neck became overwhelming.

But she couldn't let go. Something inside her pushed harder. With her free hand, she punched out at Harvey's gut. But the man was like stone. The blows had no effect except to tighten his grip further.

A darkness crept in at the edge of Gabriella's sight. She continued to punch and continued to squeeze. Something inside forced her to try. But without oxygen, her efforts grew weaker.

The final punch Gabriella delivered was feeble. The squeeze she had on him softened to nothing, and her hand dropped to the floor to support her toppling weight. She looked up at him, his eyes black, his stare neutral, offering neither a look of compassion nor hatred.

As the envelope of darkness closed on her sight like black curtains and a rush of cold blood swept through her body from her toes to her head, Gabriella heard Harvey utter a single word.

"One."

———

Using a small hatchet, Harvey broke down the smashed coffee table into smaller pieces for the fire. He stacked them on the dry pile beside the log burner, burying the hatchet into a log. Then he moved into the bedroom to dress.

He found a pair of his usual black cargo pants and a white t-shirt then pulled on his tan boots and leather biker's jacket. He slipped his phone into his pocket then gave the room a quick glance and took a mental snapshot, a habit taught to him by his mentor.

In the kitchen, he filled a glass of water, found a straw in the drinks cabinet where Melody stored alcohol, then strode over to the dining table, where, bound to a chair by her arms and legs, Gabriella sat. Her head was hanging low and her eyes were closed. Only her restraints held her upright on the chair.

Half a glass of water splashed onto her face woke her with a start.

Her skin had turned white. Dark rings were forming around her eyes and her pupils were dilated, showing only a thin trace of her brown eyes. Harvey dropped the straw into the glass and held it up for her to drink.

The re-hydration did little to wake her. Though her eyes had widened, she stared at the floor with her mouth hanging open and a sweat on her brow that gave her skin a sickly sheen.

"Here's what's going to happen," said Harvey, placing his Sig on the dining table beside the glass. "I'm going to give you some clothes. You're going to freshen up, and then we're going to go for a ride. I'll drop you at the police station. Then you're on your own."

The girl offered no response. Her eyes closed and she let her head fall forward again.

A hard slap across her face woke her once more.

"You need to wake up, Gabriella."

But again, the girl just stared at the floor.

Harvey snatched his knife from his belt, slit the bindings on her wrists and ankles, and then hoisted her over his shoulder. He walked to the bathroom, lowered her to the shower floor, and set the water to cold before turning the shower on full.

Within five seconds, Gabriella was wide awake and scrambling at the wet shower walls in a confused state. Another five seconds and she was hurling abuse at Harvey, slipping on the tiles trying to get out. In five more seconds, she was out of the shower, shivering and hugging herself, until Harvey turned the water off and threw her a towel.

He stepped outside into the room, grabbed a few of Melody's old clothes, then returned to the bathroom and dropped them on the floor.

"Get dressed," said Harvey, then shut the door to give her some privacy.

A few minutes passed, which Harvey spent standing in the kitchen with his eye on the bathroom door wondering if Christmas in London with Melody, Tyler, Jess and Reg would have been easier. Then the door opened. Gabriella emerged looking refreshed and clean, wearing a pair of Melody's track bottoms and one of Harvey's white t-shirts, which hung from Gabriella's small frame like she'd borrowed her big sister's clothes.

She stopped in the hallway, her bottom lip sucked into her mouth and a sorrowful look in her eye.

"There's a pair of running shoes by the door. They should fit. You can have them," said Harvey.

"Merci," said Gabriella, as she made her way past Harvey, giving him a wide berth.

"Call it a parting gift."

She stooped to pull on the running shoes but staggered, unsteady on her feet.

From a distance, Harvey watched but refused to help. It was as if the girl was drunk. Even when she stood up straight, the blood rushed to her head and she had to use the door frame to steady herself.

"I'll be okay," she said when she saw Harvey watching.

Harvey didn't reply. He was enjoying the silence and the thought of peace and quiet.

"How far is the police station?" asked Gabriella.

"Twenty minutes," said Harvey, then gestured for her to leave with a nod of his head.

He gave the house another quick glance, making a mental note of the room, then locked the doors. The girl staggered a little in the fresh air, hugging herself for warmth. As Harvey pushed open the garage door, she peered inside, her eyes bloodshot and dilated.

"You'll need this," said Harvey inside the garage, and he tossed Gabriella a helmet.

"You do not have a car?"

"Coming from the girl who doesn't have shoes or clothes of her own?"

"I'm sorry. I didn't mean to offend you," said Gabriella. "It's just, well, it's cold."

Harvey eyed the girl who had just broken into his house and tried to kill him. She averted her eyes, apparently embarrassed by her comment.

With a sigh, Harvey removed his Sig from his jacket and tucked it into his waistband. He fixed his knife to his belt then slid out of his jacket and tossed it to her. Then he turned the key in the motorbike's ignition. It started on the first turn of the starter and idled with a low rumble.

"Have you ever been on a bike?" asked Harvey as he climbed on.

A long slender leg in ill-fitting track pants slid over the seat behind him and Gabriella's hands found Harvey's torso.

"There's a lot of things I hadn't done until today," she replied, her French accent becoming clearer.

"Is that right?" said Harvey, pulling his helmet on and sliding the visor down. "Like what?"

"Running from a pack of dogs, being hunted by armed guards in a helicopter, breaking into a house, and attacking a man with a knife. To name a few."

Harvey turned on his seat with one foot on the ground. She stared back at him through the open visor and shrugged.

"Just saying," she said.

"Hold on tight. Lean when I lean and keep your mouth shut," said Harvey. "And if you try anything stupid, men in helicopters will be the least of your trouble."

"So how do you think they got out?" asked Jones, as he and Kane stepped from the control room, closing the door to quieten Farrow's weak threats.

"It's interesting. I worked it out as soon as I learned how Doctor Goldsborough died," said Kane, letting his number two struggle with the answer for a moment. Kane delighted in demonstrating his superior brain power. He walked with his hands behind his back, a method to improve his posture with the added benefit of appearing relaxed even in the most trying of times. "The girl convinced him to do it."

"The girl? But she was in the locked room."

"You heard Farrow's complaints when we were in the

control room. Did you hear him banging on the glass? Did you notice how clear his voice was?"

Jones nodded.

"Imagine. It's the middle of the night, and all you can hear are the seductive tones of a bright young female who is just a few feet in front of you. Maybe she let him see a little skin. Maybe she gave him a show. The doctors have it wrong. To them, the observation room is a window into the minds of the test subjects. But you heard him say it. If the body doesn't trigger the adrenaline, the drug waits. Dormant. Until withdrawal kicks in. The same goes for the brain. It's a muscle. Given the right stimuli, who knows what a person is capable of when the drug kicks in. For the right mind, that pane of glass is a window into the mind of whoever is sitting in the control room, late at night, alone, with just two pretty girls to look at."

"You mean, like a superior intelligence?"

"Exactly. All it would take would be for the girl to get the doctor talking. She'd be searching for a crack in his armour. A way in. But when she found it, with the right questions and feminine persuasion, who knows what she could get the doctor to do?"

"You think she convinced him to swallow his tongue?" said Jones. "Using just words?"

"Using her mind, Jones," said Kane. He stopped at the lab room where, on the white tables inside, sitting in neat rows, sat hundreds of vials of deep red liquid. The vials were in batches of five in plastic containers. "You see, Jones, the drug was designed to enhance every aspect of human performance. It takes brain power as well as sheer brawn and determination to win a war, you know?"

"So by giving her the drug but removing the chance of exercise or adrenaline, the drug concentrates on the brain?" asked Jones, struggling to understand.

"Yes. If the human body isn't active. For example, when you're at home watching TV, your brain is still working. It's the most active muscle in the human body," said Kane. "Even yours, Jones. The energy has to go somewhere."

"That only explains how she killed the doctor. How did she get out?"

"I think I know the answer to that too," said Kane, nodding at Farrow down the corridor, who was pressed against the glass, staring at them.

"You think Farrow let her out?"

Kane nodded.

"Why would he do that?" said Jones.

"You want to know what I think?" said Kane. "I think Farrow fell for the girl's charm. He's weak. He made a mistake and he's covering his tracks."

"You think the girl convinced him to let her go?"

"I don't know, Jones," said Kane. "But I do know that Farrow's usefulness has come to an end."

Jones stared back at Farrow, who looked at them, trying to work out if he'd been rumbled.

"We need to find her before the prime minister arrives," said Kane. "He'll be driving into town at six a.m. By that time, I want the girl dead and I want your men in position. Is that clear, Jones?"

"Farrow mentioned withdrawal symptoms. How dangerous is this girl?"

"She'll be weakening. She'll be begging for a fix. Lure her out with a fix of the cheap stuff," said Kane, gesturing at the rows of prototype vials in the adjacent room. "Do whatever it takes. But do not come back here without her and the finished product that she stole."

Jones nodded.

"In thirty-six hours' time, the French prime minister will be making his way to Saint-Pierre for his annual holiday on his yacht. This is our chance at redemption. It might be the last one we get. If we fail, we'll live the rest of our lives in hiding, and I don't know about you, Jones, but I'm tired of living in hiding. I'm tired of disgrace. I want the world to see how strong we are."

"We only have twenty men, sir."

"You're right," said Kane, as he stared through a window at the rows of vials in a temperature controlled room. "But twenty highly trained men pumped full of SFS will be a formidable force."

"Charlie-two, this is Victor-one," said a tinny voice over Jones' radio, which was clipped to his belt. "We have a positive ID on the girl."

The attention of both men was caught. Jones reached for the radio.

"Victor-one, this is Charlie-two. Go ahead."

"The dogs picked up her scent. We traced it to a small farmhouse on the coast. But there's no sign of her."

"Do you think she's got help?" Jones asked.

"I don't know, sir. It's hard to say. The trail ends here."

Kane took the radio from Jones and held it up to his mouth.

"Victor-one, this is Charlie-one."

"Sir?"

"Search the property. Find me the missing vial. Charlie-two will enlist the help of the local police. She can't have gone far."

"Copy," said Victor-one. "Will that be all, sir?"

"No," said Kane. "Destroy the house. Leave no trace."

5

RUN LIKE HELL

"Is this it?" asked Gabriella, as Harvey pulled the bike to a stop on the beach road.

They sat two hundred yards from the police station, which was a single-floor, whitewashed building with shuttered windows and two weather-beaten, wooden front doors. The grounds were un-tended with long grass on both sides of the dirt track and fruit-bearing trees spilling their produce onto the ground below.

"What was you expecting? This isn't London or Paris. It's the French coast. Nothing happens here."

Outside the police station were two old Peugeot police cars and a black SUV with mud spattered up the sides of the paintwork. The Peugeots were parked in the shade beside the building. The SUV looked out of place as if it belonged to a visitor who had just stopped without parking and left the car to make a statement.

"So you're just going to leave me here?" said Gabriella, feeling a wave of nausea climb to the back of her throat, then recede when she swallowed.

Harvey didn't reply.

"Can you take me to the door at least?"

"The ride ends here," said Harvey. He revved the engine once, a single blast of the exhaust to demonstrate his impatience.

"Okay, okay. I got it," said Gabriella, as she slid from the bike.

She pulled off the helmet and let her long hair hang free. But the show didn't distract Harvey. He remained with his visor down and his eyes set on the door of the police station as if he expected to be rushed by the men inside at any minute.

"Do you have a history with them?" asked Gabriella, feeling her cheeks whiten; sleep beckoned.

Harvey shook his head.

"There's more to you than meets the eye, isn't there, Harvey Stone?" said Gabriella, fighting nausea with deep breaths. "I get the impression that you've tucked yourself away in that little farmhouse for a reason. You're hiding from something."

Harvey snatched the helmet from her hands, leaned back, and dropped it into the back box.

"Jacket?" said Harvey.

"Are you really going to leave a girl all the way out here with nothing but a t-shirt and pants?"

Harvey didn't reply.

"I guess you are," said Gabriella. She slid the jacket from her arms. "And they say chivalry is dead."

"Are we done?" asked Harvey, pulling his jacket on and connecting the zipper.

"I guess we are," said Gabriella. "I'd love to say it was nice meeting you-"

Before Gabriella could finish her sentence, Harvey dropped the bike into first gear. He checked the mirror and accelerated off onto the quiet beach road, leaving her to watch him ride away with just the glittering reflection of the Mediterranean by his side and a dark and stormy sky above.

"Goodbye, Harvey Stone," Gabriella said to herself, watching him fade to a tiny dot at the end of the road. She turned and began the short walk to the police station, going over what she planned to say in her head.

The building was small, a one-story cube with only a few small windows to keep the inside cool. It sat on a piece of wasteland, a baron collection of hard-packed gravel that allowed only the most resilient of weeds and grasses to climb their way into the sun. Behind and to one side, in stark contrast to the moon-like surface of the police station grounds, was the edge of the forest. Gabriella felt as if the land surrounding the police station had succumbed to the negative energy and corruption that grew like wildfire inside the building. It was, in Gabriella's mind, tainted land.

A single policeman sat behind a single counter that offered no bulletproof glass to shield him from an attack. Only an old electric fan sat with him, either to keep him cool or keep the flies away. A line of eight old wooden chairs ran across one wall. But Gabriella doubted that any more than two or three had ever been occupied at any one time.

The cop behind the desk followed her with his eyes as she approached. He sat with one leg folded over the other and a newspaper resting on his lap. Judging by the man's waistline, he hadn't seen much heavy action in recent years. A man's laugh came from the room behind him. There was an office maybe and perhaps a cell for rogue, drunk tourists. A single door behind the counter was its only exit.

"I'd like to report a kidnapping," said Gabriella. "Do you speak English?"

The cop just stared up at her from his seat. He allowed his eyes to wander to her chest before they returned to meet her stare. Making a show of closing his newspaper, he sat forward, leaned on the desk and collected a pen from a stationary pot, which, Gabriella noted, held just one pen.

"Quel est votre nom?" said the cop.

"Anglais?"

But the cop just stared back at her as if the thought of speaking English offended him.

"Gabriella," she said.

Again, the man stared up at her, waiting for a full response.

"Gabriella DuBois," said Gabriella. "D.U.B.O.I.S. DuBois."

"Date de naissance?"

"Did you hear what I said?" said Gabriella. "I'd like to report a kidnapping. I don't have time to-"

"Date de naissance?" the cop repeated, cutting her off.

"July fifth."

"En Francais."

"Le cinq juillet."

"Annee?"

"Quatre vingt onze."

"Bien," said the policeman, placing his pen back into the empty pot. He sat back and linked his fingers across his ample stomach. "Comment puis-je t'aider?"

"These men..." she began. Then she felt a warm sting of tears welling in her eyes and held onto the chair for support. Still, the cop stared at her, offering little assistance. She took a breath. "They kidnapped..."

But as she began to tell her story to the lazy cop behind the counter, the men's voices in the back room grew louder.

"I ran all night," said Gabriella.

But the voices. She singled out one in particular then stared at the door in disbelief.

"That voice."

"Madam?" the cop prompted her.

But Gabriella began to step backwards, moving away from

the desk, away from the cop. Even before the door handle turned, she knew who would step through the frame.

"Madam," called the cop, standing from his chair, confused by her reaction. "Où allez-vous?"

Three men, all bearing smiles, emerged from the back room. But the look on the desk officer's face and his raised voice had caught their attention.

The first man, a senior policeman with a gut larger than his deputy's, switched his confused look between Gabriella and the second man, who was wearing black pants and black boots, and cocked his head to one side.

"You," said Jones.

"No," said Gabriella, shaking her head. She bumped into the door, struggling to open it.

"Get after her," shouted Jones.

Man number three leapt into action.

Barging through the doors into the bright daylight, Gabriella looked left then right and found an opening in the forest. Behind her, as she ran, the doors crashed open and the third man gave chase. Tears leaked from her eyes and streamed across her face, pushed back by the wind. With her arms pumping as hard as they could, Gabriella prayed for the warm lick of whatever it was they had injected into her to rush across her muscles.

But nothing came but fatigue.

A gunshot rang out. The bullet found the bark of a tree and ricocheted off with a high-pitched whine. But Gabriella kept running. Soon, the only sound she could hear was the dull beat of her heart. She focused on one step after the other, leaping over logs and streams until the trees grew so dense she had to slow to cut a path between them.

Thick bushes sat at the feet of tall pines. The ground was a carpet of dry pine cones and scattered with leaves of autumn colour. Stopping behind a thick trunk, Gabriella calmed her heart and listened to the movement around her, forming an image in her mind of her hunter.

The heavy footfalls slowed to a stop. She imagined the man with his gun held out before him, sweeping the rows of trees for a sign of her. As the footfalls came closer, Gabriella prepared herself. The muzzle of the gun emerging from behind the thick pine trunk was the sign she needed.

With two hands, she reached out, twisting the gun and disabling the man's hands with his finger stuck in the trigger guard. A shot fired off and a small pile of leaves exploded on the ground beside her. The first blow the man threw was with an elbow. With his hands stuck on the gun, it was all he could manage, along with a sweep of his legs to knock Gabriella off balance.

But Gabriella was ready for the move. Using every ounce of energy that remained in her tired body, she ducked from the elbow and fell forward, pulling the man down as he swept his leg across. He came down hard on top of her, but momentum kept them rolling until they came to a stop with Gabriella on top, one knee on each of his shoulders.

She eased her knee forward onto his neck, squeezing his windpipe. With his hands still locked on the gun, Gabriella gave everything she had to close the man's airway, pulling his arms up and away and her knee down, hard on his throat.

The choking sounds and rustle of dead leaves fell quiet and the silence of the forest resumed. The man's hands fell limp, allowing Gabriella to release the gun.

A single shot to his head confirmed he was dead.

Breathless from the exertion and tension, Gabriella fell sideways to the ground, lying beside the man she had just killed.

Tears formed in her eyes and the harder she fought them, the more they formed until she relented to the emotions that had built up over the past two days. She curled into a ball and wept. Alone in a forest with nowhere to go and no-one even looking for her, she pitied herself. Even the birds in the tree-tops ceased their singing. The occasional branch flicked as a squirrel leapt to another tree. But no other sound followed.

Until, someplace far off, somewhere behind many trees and across a carpet of dead leaves and dried pine cones...

That voice called out.

Being a man of healthy routine and good habits, Harvey parked his bike in the detached garage, turned it around and killed the engine. He stepped off the bike, pulled off his helmet and slipped it into the soft helmet cover. Then he pulled the drawstring tight and hung the bag with the helmet inside on a single hook on the wall.

He entered the house through the back door as he always did, and scanned the room. It was a subconscious glance rather than a thorough investigation. Practice had taught him to leave items on surfaces perfectly square with their surroundings. Any movement or variation would stand out and catch his eye.

The iron fire tools had been moved.

Standing in the doorway, he studied the fire iron from fifteen feet away, thinking back to the fight he'd had with Gabriella. Had he moved them? Or hadn't he returned the iron to its place? But his confidence in his own methods far outweighed his doubt. Any discrepancy in the iron's position would have been noticed when he left the house with Gabriella.

With one quiet and smooth motion, he pulled the gun from his waistband and armed it, releasing the slide as quietly as possible. Even from the doorway, he could see the door to the bathroom in the hallway was slightly ajar. Another sign.

He stepped into the room, closing the kitchen door behind him, and walked through the hallway.

With the gun aimed at chest height, Harvey snatched the door open.

But nobody was there.

He glanced into the bedroom. The wardrobe had been ransacked. The drawers had been pulled out and emptied onto the floor. The contents of every box and bag was strewn across the bed.

A flash of light pulsed behind his eyes. Inside Harvey's gut, something stirred. The familiar feeling of his inner beast opened its eyes.

A dull thud came from the kitchen. It was the sound of the kitchen door closing.

"Gabriella?" said Harvey, trying hard to control the rage growing inside him.

But no reply came.

A shape passed by the kitchen window, quick and dark. Standing in the bedroom, Harvey traced the runner with his Sig. A flash of black against the bright sun behind, as the intruder passed by the living room window. Harvey continued to track him from the hallway. Then, as the muzzle of the gun lined up with the bedroom window, he fired.

Glass shattered and fell to the floor, and the moans of the intruder squirming on the ground came through the broken window.

Rolling his neck from side to side, feeling the click of bones, muscle and the release gases in his joints, Harvey made his way outside.

He slid the Sig into his waistband, stepped outside the house, and found the man lying on the ground beside Harvey's wood shelter, a small wooden lean-to frame he'd built the previous summer to keep his supply of wood dry.

Inside the lean-to was the neat stack of firewood Harvey had been maintaining, along with an axe and a hatchet.

With one hand on the man's collar and the other on his belt, Harvey hoisted him into the air and slammed him into the wall of his house. The intruder's back bent across the wood pile. Fuelled by rage, Harvey held the man in black high above his head with his toes scratching the concrete ground. He slammed the man's face into the brickwork over and over until he could hold him no more, and let him drop to the ground.

A boot to the man's ribs rolled him onto his back, where Harvey could study his bloodied face. But he didn't recognise the man with one swollen eye, a broken nose and a claret-stained beard.

"Who are you and what are you doing in my house?" said Harvey, with his boot on the bullet wound in the man's shoulder.

But the man failed to respond. He made no effort to talk. Instead, he moaned at his injuries and stared up at Harvey with his one good eye.

"I'll ask you again. Who are you?" said Harvey.

But the man only smiled. The beginnings of a laugh came out but it was drowned in a cough thick with blood.

Hoisting the man to his feet, Harvey forced him against the wall inside the lean-to. He pulled his knife from the sheave on his belt, and put the blade against the man's throat, before searching his jacket and finding a wallet.

There was a European driver's license with the name Frederick Shaw.

"Tell me what you're doing here," said Harvey, tossing the wallet and the license to the ground. "You're not a burglar. You're looking for something."

No reply came.

"You came to the wrong house, Freddie," said Harvey. "You just pissed off the wrong guy."

He dug his thumb into the bullet wound, savouring the man's face twisting in agony. Spittle flew from Freddie's mouth as he fought the urge to scream. So Harvey dug harder, searching inside for the taut feel of tendons until he heard the scream he was anticipating.

The scream came and Freddie's knees buckled.

"You're going to tell me what you're looking for," said Harvey.

But still, he received no response other than a dry smile and a weak, bloodied laugh.

Harvey grabbed the man's arm, lay his hand flat on the wooden frame of the lean-to and, with one slick arc of his arm, he stabbed the blade through the man's hand, fixing him to the wood. A growl came from the very depths of Freddie. His breathing was short and shallow as if he were hyperventilating.

Harvey collected the hatchet from where it hung between two four-inch nails. He ran the blade across Freddie's shoulder as if deciding where to place the first cut.

Freddie's eyes opened wide, fearful of the hatchet and the lunatic who wielded it. It was a sign Harvey had seen a hundred times before a hundred confessions. He dropped the blade to the man's elbow.

"Elbow or shoulder," said Harvey. "Your choice."

The confident arrogance had vanished from Freddie's demeanour. He searched Harvey's eyes for a sign of weakness, a sign that he wouldn't go through with it.

But Harvey offered no such sign.

"I'll decide then, shall I?"

Harvey swung the hatchet back, but just as it reached the apex of the swing, Freddie spoke.

"The girl."

Harvey stopped. But he held the hatchet high, mid-swing. "What girl?"

"The girl that came here this morning."

Harvey didn't reply.

"We know she came here. Our dogs picked up her scent."

"Who do you work for?"

But Freddie just laughed. This time, it was loud and with renewed confidence.

Harvey completed his swing of the hatchet and buried the blade into the man's shoulder.

A wild scream rang out, and as Harvey lined up for his second swing, the agonised yelp evolved into another laugh. It was the laugh of a madman.

Freddie closed his eyes, laid his head back, and smiled up at the sky.

It was only then that Harvey noticed the wood pile. The top row was missing four logs, something Harvey almost never let happen. Only one row was taken inside at a time. Never one or two logs. Never half a row. Always a full row.

Freddie caught Harvey staring at the wood, and once more, his laugh filled the small space in the lean-to.

An image of the living room came back to Harvey.

He'd opened the kitchen door.

The fire irons had been moved.

The open bathroom door.

The blazing fire.

The logs should have burned down to coals. But there was a blazing fire.

As the realisation of what Freddie had done hit Harvey, Freddie erupted into uncontrollable laughter. Harvey stepped back and looked across at the house.

Smoke had begun to billow out of the windows and orange flames licked at the curtains.

The beast inside Harvey woke from its slumber. A surge

of power pulsed behind his eyes. Sharp talons of the beast gripped his insides and, in a rare state of uncontrolled anger, he swung the hatchet back and aimed at Freddie's chest.

But it was too late.

The side of the house exploded in a shower of bricks, splintered wood and angry flames.

"It's just you and me, Doctor Farrow," said Kane, as he lowered himself into the seat and released the microphone button. Farrow's hands slid from the glass and hung limply by his sides. Somewhere on his face was an expression of hate, camouflaged by wonder, intrigue and a lack of understanding.

"Why?" said Farrow. "Why have me create all this and then moments before we finish, you destroy it all?"

"I'm not destroying it, Doctor Farrow. I thought that much was clear."

"If you kill me, you won't stand a chance," said Farrow. His voice had lost its urgency, as if his heart had resolved to his new prison. He spoke in gentle tones. "Only I know how to finish the project."

"The project *is* finished, Doctor Farrow," said Kane. He laid his hands on his lap and stared back at the doctor, offering him a look of compassion and disappointment. "Tell me straight. Where's the undiluted SFS?"

"I told you, I don't know. She must have stolen it when she escaped," said Farrow. But his expression betrayed his own deceit.

"Don't take me for a fool," said Kane.

"You're wrong. I've been nothing but faithful to you," snapped Farrow. "Even when you erupted into your little tantrums, shoved people around and set unrealistic expectations, who do you think stood by you? I defended you when the rest of the scientists and technicians threatened to leave. Who do you think kept this project alive? And now you repay me with this? A glass prison?"

"Be careful, Mr Farrow," said Kane, and he smoothed his lock of grey hair back into place.

"No. No, I damn well won't. If this is how you treat the people that help you, then I'll have nothing more to do with you. I'll have nothing more to do with the project. You can't use it. It's still untested. We still have weeks of research to do."

"The drug works, Doctor Farrow. We've seen it time and again. How much longer do I have to wait?"

"The drug works during physical activity, yes. But what about the dormant hosts? You saw what the girl did. Who knows what else she's capable of? We need to test it. We need to research and we need to make adjustments to the formula. You can't just inject people with it as it is. Not in the real world. There's too much uncertainty. And what is it you plan on doing with it anyway? You never did say. You can't sell it to the military. The research would never stand up."

"I'm not selling it to the military, Doctor Farrow."

"So who?" said Farrow. He began to pace the room. "Just let me out. Let me finish the job."

"Did I ever tell you about the time my father locked me in the cellar, Doctor Farrow?"

The doctor stopped pacing. He stared through the window, incredulous at the remark.

"What does that have to do with this? You're killing people, Kane. If this gets out into the wrong hands, there'll be chaos."

"I was an only child, you see. We lived on an old farm. It was a dream of my father's, I think, to have all that land. All that space. My mother went along for the ride. Back then, they did that, didn't they? Wives. There was no equality. If the woman spoke up against her husband, she'd be beaten. At least in our household, that's how it was. You see, my father was quite mad, I think. He was never diagnosed, but the signs were there, in hindsight. And me, a boy with all the time and space to exercise my curiosity as boys do, I was fascinated by the circle of life. How the birds ate the seeds my father planted, no matter how much it infuriated him." Kane smiled at the memory of his father's temper. "Then, through some kind of magic, the droppings of those birds would spread the seed. Somehow, through the miracle of life, that seed had sustained that little bird, given it energy and all the things it needed to live another day, and still, it had the power to bring more life, growing a new plant wherever that little bird happened to drop it. Quite fascinating. Don't you think, Doctor Farrow?"

"I'm a scientist," replied Farrow. His voice was low and calm as he pictured the little boy in Kane's anecdote.

"So I trapped one," said Kane. "You know the trick? A box held up with a stick and a piece of string. I sat there all day waiting for one to come along. And I nearly gave up too. But it's amazing what a little willpower can do."

"You caught one?" asked Farrow.

"I wrung its neck in my tiny hands, just as I'd seen my father do with the chickens. I felt the life leave its tiny body and I held it up to see it in the fading sunlight. I marvelled at how light it felt. How delicate life is. I sneaked back to my room and used a small kitchen knife to open it up. How wonderful life is, Doctor Farrow. It's a miracle how all those tiny organs fit into that little body."

There was a pause as Kane relived the moment when his life had changed. But, feeling Farrow's eyes on him, silently waiting for the next part of the story, he continued.

"Curiosity got the better of me, I'm afraid. It wasn't long before I was opening up the feral cats on the farm. I was fascinated by the intricacies of their bodies, but naive to think that my parents wouldn't notice the smell of their rotting corpses in my cupboard."

"Your father found them?" asked Farrow.

"My mother found them. But being the devoted wife she was, she went straight to my father. She was fearful I was turning into a monster."

"And were you?"

"No," said Kane. "I was never a monster, Doctor Farrow. I was just a boy who was fascinated by the physical body. My father locked me in the cellar for three days straight with no food or water. No sunlight. Only the rats to keep me company. That's where it all began, Doctor Farrow. So when you talk about your research and what our little creation can do to a man's mind, I already know. I already know the possibilities of the human mind. I realised it on the seventh day of being locked in that little cellar. The curious rats with their tiny claws and teeth woke me every ten minutes. And the darkness, Farrow, darkness like you've never experienced before. They say your eyes adjust to the dark after time. But not when that darkness is total. When you're so far underground that your fingertips are bleeding from scratching at the walls and the door. Your forehead is swollen from trying to end it all, just to stop the incessant rats and torturous squeals and bites. All you want to do is say you're sorry. Seven days, Doctor Farrow, that's how long it took. When my body was at its weakest, my mind was broken, and death hung over me licking his lips, that's when I found it. That's when I found the strength to get out. That's when I became the man I am now. With nothing but a few meagre slices of stale bread that I had to share with the rats and a few cups of water from the drain, I found the strength to break free."

"You escaped?" asked Farrow.

"I did more than escape, Farrow. You never saw a boy so alive, so strong and fearsome."

"That's why you want the drug? That's the basis of all this research?"

"I know, Doctor Farrow, that the human body is capable of so much more. Instinct protects us. But what if it didn't? What could man be capable of if the measures that nature gave us to harvest energy, to feel fatigue, and to protect ourselves from ruination were removed? I know, Farrow. I know what they are. I know that just ten men with unlimited power, led by a man such as myself, would be unstoppable."

"You're as mad as your father, Kane," said Farrow. "You'll kill them all. All this will be for nothing. Let me help you. Let me finish the research."

"Oh, you're going to finish the research, Doctor Farrow," said Kane, taking delight in the relief that washed over his face. "In the absence of another suitable test subject, you're going to be my final experiment."

6

TRAMPLED UNDERFOOT

"I'll find you," called Jones.

That voice.

"I gave you a chance once before and you blew it. You chose to run."

Dead leaves beneath his feet crunched as he circled the dead body on the ground. Fifteen feet away, Gabriella hugged the trunk of a pine, not daring to move.

"The truth is, Gabriella, you need us. What are you going to do when it runs out? What are you going to do when your body aches for more? When you can no longer function without it? Doctor Farrow told me all about the symptoms."

His words elicited a desire in Gabriella's body; a bead of sweat formed on her brow. The skin on her back burned as if a fire roared in her flesh. Her throat, as parched as the desert sand, seemed to shrivel and crack like the leaves beneath her feet.

"What are you going to do, Gabriella?" His rough London accent conveyed the charmless smile of a man who held all the cards. "I have what you want right here. Do you want me to ease your pain? I can do it, Gabriella. I can make you strong again."

A shuffle of leaves scattered and his voice quietened as he moved away. Gabriella rested her forehead against the bark of the tree. She stared at her hand. Her fingers twitched as if electricity pulsed through her veins. Her peripheral darkened and no matter how many times she blinked away the tears, her vision remained a blur.

"I'm leaving now, Gabriella. The choice is yours. If you want help, if you want what I have, then you come and find me. I'll be waiting."

A fatigue, stronger than ever before, came over Gabriella, weakening her legs. She clung to the tree but her fingers failed to grasp the bark. A wave of nausea washed through her body. Her burning skin and cold sweat found the forest breeze and she fell to the forest floor, breathless.

"Wait," she called out between gasps of air, using what felt like every ounce of remaining energy in her body. She squeezed her eyes closed as a rush of blood swelled behind her eyes. Then she crawled to the tree and lay against it as sleep seeped into her mind like dark molasses.

The crunching of leaves stopped.

"Show yourself, Gabriella," called Jones. "Show me you're not armed."

"I am armed," she called, and she felt the rise of acid at the back of her parched throat. "But I can't run any further."

"What about the vial that Farrow gave you? That's right, Gabriella, we know all about Farrow and the finished product."

"I don't have it."

"You used it already?" said the man. "No. I don't believe that for a second. You'd be high as a kite by now."

"I've hidden it. Somewhere safe," said Gabriella. "Somewhere you'll never find it. If you kill me, it'll be gone forever."

"Very clever, Gabriella."

"It's my insurance. Give me a hit and I'll tell you where it is," said Gabriella. She spat the putrid acid from her mouth. A string of thick liquid hung from her lip, but she no longer had the energy to care. "I just need one more hit of the prototype to help me walk."

"And then what?" said the man. "You take a dose and run again? Is that it? What about when that runs out?"

"It looks like you're the one with choices now, Jones. Option one," she called, recalling the choices he had given her the previous night. "You give me a hit of the prototype in your pocket. I walk out of here and tell you where to find the undiluted SFS."

"That's risky," said Jones. "Not much of an option. What's option two?"

"I put this gun to my head and you deal with the consequences."

The dust was still settling but the fire had exhausted anything combustible by the time Harvey came around. The roof of the garage laid on top of him. It was a single sheet of corrugated asbestos burdened with the weight of loose bricks and timbers pinning him to the ground.

He flexed his fingers and toes before trying to move his arms. Then he found room for his legs to move. But with nothing solid within reach, there was no purchase to push or pull himself out from the debris.

A small gap in the rubble to his right allowed a slither of sunlight to reach his face. He turned his head, seeking fresh air and feeling the weight of the roof on his chest as it rose and fell. But the stale, acrid air of fire smoke and dust was all he found.

He tried to roll, forcing the asbestos sheet up just a few inches, enough to make room for his body to shift onto his front. A wound in his leg screamed out at him, and the familiar warm trickle of blood cooled on his skin. With the smallest movements of his toes against the concrete, he worked his way toward a hole in the rubble, clearing debris to widen the gap as he crawled. Harvey's injured leg trailed behind, limp like a dead companion being dragged from the battlefield. With just his elbows and one foot, Harvey scraped, pulled and pushed until, at last, his head emerged through the hole in the ruins.

To force his arms through the gap meant the full weight of the roof crushed his chest. Eventually his hands, searching blindly in the open air, found a timber to hold. With a final pull, he wrenched himself free of the rubble.

Harvey rolled to one side, holding his damaged leg off the ground. Looking down, he found a shard of timber sticking from his thigh. His pants were torn and soaked with blood. He pulled the tear wider, exposing the wound, and reeled with pain as he inspected the damaged flesh.

With gritted teeth, he growled loudly as he worked the wood from his leg. Then, when the shard came free, he rolled onto his back, breathing deep and long, controlling the pain.

It was only when the initial sting of the injury had passed that Harvey opened his eyes, wiped them with the sleeve of his jacket and dared to look at what remained of his house. The entire side wall had blown out. The lack of support had collapsed the roof, which had fallen into the house and destroyed everything Harvey owned. The blaze from the explosion had burned through the ancient roof trusses, leaving just three half-standing walls and a pile of bricks and tiles.

Deep inside Harvey, another fire raged.

A brick moved close by then fell to the concrete floor

followed by a shower of dust. A hand appeared from the far side of the debris pile, followed by an arm, coated in dust and blood. Freddie fought to scramble free of the debris, dislodging a pile of roof tiles that slid and crashed to the ground.

Rolling to his good leg, Harvey pushed himself onto one knee, wincing at the stab of pain in his thigh. He found a length of old window frame that had been ripped out of the house by the blast. Two long, twisted, rusty nails protruded from one end. With the help of the timber, and by keeping his leg straight, Harvey managed to get to his feet. Then he hopped, dragging his foot behind him, toward the noise.

Half-buried under a pile of roof tiles and broken bricks, Freddie clambered free. Blood dripped from his forehead and neck. His leg was twisted at an unnatural angle and dragged behind him as Harvey's did. But Freddie's showed a glint of white bone through the broken skin.

Harvey swung the timber and buried the nails into the man's shoulder, eliciting a scream, long and loud. With gritted teeth and fighting to control the anger raging inside him, Harvey dragged Freddie away from the rubble. Then he dropped down onto one knee and rolled him onto his back, where he stared at Harvey with the same defiant amusement he had shown before.

"Tell me who you work for and I'll end it now," said Harvey, easing his own leg straight to stem the bleeding.

But the man merely coughed a spray of bloodied mist.

"And if I don't?" said Freddie, his voice choked with blood.

"I'll break every bone in your body."

But Freddie said nothing, forcing a smug smile between rasping breaths.

Finding a broken brick close by, Harvey took it in one

hand, and without warning, he slammed it down onto the man's arm, crushing the bone against the concrete. Freddie's head shot up, but with Harvey kneeling on his chest, all he could do was growl and spit as the pain took hold of him.

"I'll ask again," said Harvey, adjusting the brick for a better grip. "Who do you work for?"

The intruder began to hyperventilate. His eyes forced shut and from deep inside him, a noise emerged, somewhere between a growl and a high-pitched whine.

Harvey brought the brick down on his other arm, feeling it crack. He held the brick in place for a moment, pushing the flesh against the shards of sharp bone and pinning the man down by his throat, who thrashed and tried to buck Harvey off his body.

But still, despite the sobs, whines and panting, the man refused to talk.

Reaching back, Harvey dropped the brick, took hold of the intruder's twisted leg by the ankle and held on as bone found nerve, and pulses of energy sent the man into spasms. His back arched, and as Harvey twisted the leg further and further, feeling the sinew stretch and tear, the man finally caved with a scream like a child. Blood leaked from his mouth. It spattered across his face and, as he lifted his head at Harvey, growling like a wild dog, it filled the gaps between his teeth.

Harvey raised the timber, resting the two sharp and bloodied points of the rusted nails on the man's forehead. Then he grabbed the brick from the ground.

Their eyes locked. The intruder stared at Harvey, pleading with his eyes to end it.

"Every man breaks at some point," said Harvey, his tone calm and soft. He spoke as a father might when sharing a nugget of wisdom with his son. "Most men will talk at the very fear of pain. Some men will wait a little longer, testing to see how far I'll push them. Others will hold out until they stare death in the eyes. Then they face the last decision they'll ever make."

"You're sick," spat Freddie, his throat thick with blood and his voice hoarse from screaming.

"The truth is, most men are weak. Most will cry. It doesn't matter how big they are. They'll cry like the day they were born at the very thought of the pain they might endure. You've done well, Freddie. You've lasted until the end," said Harvey, eying the two nails as they formed tiny dents in the man's forehead. "But this isn't the end. If you're thinking that all of this will be over in a few moments, if you're thinking you only have to hold on for a short while, think again, Freddie."

"Just do it," said Freddie. Then he lowered his voice as he faced his destiny. "Just finish me."

"I can make it stop," said Harvey, his voice quiet but loud enough to be heard above the panting. "Just say the words and it'll all be over."

"You'll never stop him," said Freddie. "He's too powerful."

"Power? Do you want to see power?" said Harvey. A flash of blood pulsed behind his eyes. He raised the brick high above him, locked eyes with the intruder, and felt the body tense beneath him. "You asked for this."

"Kane," said Freddie. "Cassius Kane."

Harvey stopped with the brick held high above his head.

"Where do I find him?"

A tear rolled from Freddie's eye, leaving a trail of pink skin in its wake, bright against his grimy face.

"Talk to me, Freddie. Where do I find him?" said Harvey.

But Freddie didn't reply.

He stared at the sky, still and silent. The rasping breaths

stopped. The grunts as he fought to control the pain throughout his body silenced.

Harvey lowered the brick in his hand. He removed the wood with the two nails from Freddie's forehead and tossed the makeshift weapons onto the debris. But only when he climbed to his feet and began to hobble away did he heard a sound.

He turned and faced the dead man.

A radio on Freddie's belt crackled into life.

"Charlie-one, this is Charlie-two. Target is recovered. I'm bringing her in."

"Take the syringe, Doctor Farrow," said Kane. "You know what to do."

The doctor's eyes shifted from the stainless steel tray of loaded syringes on the trolley to Kane, who sat in the control room behind the glass. His feet rested on the desk and his hands laid folded on his lap as if he were watching a movie.

The show was just beginning.

"No," said Farrow. "I'm not a lab rat. I'm not one of your kidnapped test subjects. I am Doctor Jeremiah Farrow. I'm one of the most respected experts in my field."

"And now you're going to demonstrate what you can do, Doctor Farrow," said Kane. "I want to see the very limits of your wonderful creation. And who better to show me than the creator?"

"You can't force me," said Farrow. "Bring me one of your prisoners."

"You are my prisoner, Farrow. Do I need to remind you that you killed three of them and let two escape? So now, it's just you."

"I didn't kill them. You can't put that on me."

"There's five syringes on that tray, Doctor Farrow. On my command, you will inject the first syringe," said Kane. He flicked the power on the video camera and hit record. "The final test, Doctor Farrow. Are you ready?"

"And if I don't?"

"Oh, you will. One way or another," replied Kane.

He leaned forward and pulled a slider back on the complex control panel.

"What are you doing?" said Farrow, seeing his movements.

"Oh, I'm just giving you a choice, Doctor Farrow. I'm not an evil man, as you know."

The hum of the ventilation fans slowed then faded to silence.

"The ventilation," said Farrow. "What have you done?"

"I would suggest perhaps remaining as calm as you can, Doctor Farrow. You're aware, I presume, how much oxygen the human body requires?"

"Yes, I'm aware," said Farrow, eying the ventilation louvres at the top of the walls.

"Given the size of that small room, I'd say you have approximately an hour to live. Now, I'm happy to sit here and watch you suffocate. But what a waste that would be, Doctor Farrow. I'll turn it back on when you inject the first syringe."

"You're a cold bastard, Kane," said Farrow. "After every-thing I've done for you?"

"Time's ticking, Doctor."

Farrow unbuttoned his cuff, holding Kane's amused gaze in his own bitter stare.

"That a boy," said Kane with a smile, and released the MIC button.

Snatching the first syringe from the tray, Farrow prepared the injection. He released the air from the chamber, tapped the syringe to make sure no air bubbles remained, then worked his arm muscles to identify the vein.

"You never know," said Kane, more to amuse himself than spur on the doctor, "that drug with a brain like yours, you could become a *real* genius."

But to Kane's surprise, the doctor needed no more spurring on. He found the vein with the point of the syringe and administered the drug with no hesitation.

"All the way, Doctor," said Kane, watching with delight.

The syringe was pulled from the doctor's arm, and he held it up for Kane to see the empty chamber. Then he dropped it into the tray with a metallic clink.

"How do you feel?" asked Kane.

"No different," replied Farrow. "Do I get some oxygen now?"

"Sure." Kane pushed the slider up to the bare minimum until the fans kicked into life.

"So what now? Do you want me to run like the test subjects?"

"No, Doctor Farrow. I do not want you to run. I want you to stand perfectly still. I want you to think about everything you ever learned. I want you to reach into the corners of your mind and open the gates."

"You're quite mad, Kane," said Farrow. "You know that's not how the drug works."

"It worked for the girl."

"It worked for the girl because she was angry, because she'd been locked up for a month with all the time in the world to devise a plan. You want to see me escape? Do you really want me to convince you to swallow your own tongue, Kane?"

"No, Doctor Farrow. No. I do not want that. Although, it would be fun to see you try. No, Doctor Farrow. I want something quite different." He flicked his eyes to the stainless steel tray and back to Farrow. "I want to break you."

"Break me?" said Farrow.

Kane pulled down the dial for the oxygen feed.

"The next syringe, if you please, Doctor Farrow."

7

LEARNING TO FLY

"How do you feel?" asked Jones, as Gabriella removed the needle from her arm. "Are you ready to walk?"

She stared back at him, her mind clouded with foggy memories of the previous day and uncertainty along whichever path she chose.

"Like I just woke up," replied Gabriella. Then she raised the gun at Jones as he took a step towards her. "No closer."

"You got what you want. Tell me where the vial is," said Jones.

"I'll tell you where the vial is when I'm somewhere safe, or you'll shoot me here and leave my body for the rodents."

"So let's walk." Jones pointed with his gun in the direction of the police station. "Ladies first."

"Are you going to shoot me in the back?" said Gabriella, as she made her way out of the forest, feeling the drug flow through her bloodstream and bringing with it a new lease of life.

"Not yet," said Jones, following her. "You try anything and I will."

"And the missing vial?"

"I'll take my chances with that one."

"So tell me," said Gabriella. "If you're so smart, why do you work for Cassius Kane? I mean, the way I see it, the men all report to you. You're the one they respect. You're the one they follow. Not him. He's just a paycheck. Am I right?"

"You don't know what you're talking about," replied Jones. "Keep walking."

"I'm just making small talk. But I guess you don't really have what it takes, do you? You don't have that vision. All leaders have a vision, you know?"

"I've got a vision alright. I've got a vision of you lying face down in this forest with a hole in the back of your head big enough to put my fist in."

"And there it is. That, right there, is why you will never be the boss."

"I can lead. I've got a vision."

"Yes. But to Kane, you're just a hired hand. To Kane, you're dispensable," said Gabriella.

She stepped across the stream she had jumped earlier when she had been running from the man she'd killed. The familiarity of the place, however fleetingly she had passed through it, came back to her with clarity. It was like she was walking a path she had walked a thousand times.

"You don't know Kane like I do," replied Jones. "With what he's got planned, we will be rich men. Our names will be cleared. Sure, I could start my own firm. I could take my men with me. They're loyal enough. But why would I do that when Kane can offer such a bright future?"

Ducking beneath some low hanging branches, Gabriella emerged and waited for Jones to follow. He came through behind her with the gun raised. In the distance, she heard the faint rumble of a lorry passing along the quiet beach road.

"Because you're weak," said Gabriella.

"Stop right there," said Jones. He stepped closer, ramming

the muzzle of the handgun under her chin and forcing Gabriella's head back.

"I know what you're doing. I know what you did to Doctor Goldsborough. You won't get me with your mind tricks. No more talking, or I'll cut your tongue from your pretty little mouth. Do you understand me?"

"So much emotion,' said Gabriella. "Just do it. Just pull the trigger."

"No more talking."

Gabriella laughed as Jones shoved her away.

"You need me alive. You're weak, Mr Jones."

"Move," said Jones.

"There's no need for the gun," said Gabriella. "I've got what I want for now."

"Just walk."

"I'm walking. I'm walking," said Gabriella, as she ducked beneath another low branch, pushing it forward out of her way. She took a breath and waited for the perfect moment.

"And stop talking," said Jones, as he followed her through the gap.

With the gun raised once more, he came through the trees and stood up straight just as Gabriella let go of the branch.

The thick bough pinged back at exactly the right height, catching him square in the face and triggering the adrenaline that Gabriella had been teasing into play. Once more, her feet and legs no longer felt like her own. The strides she took seemed long and endless. Jones' shot, which sang out behind her, ricocheted off the trees. The clarity with which the path lay out before her was a stark contrast to the blur she experienced from withdrawal on the way into the forest.

The white police building showed through the trees on her left, and to her right, the road beside the forest was as clear as day. She leapt a final ditch before breaking from the trees and landing with both feet on the tarmac road.

A screech of tyres to her right. Then the silence that ensues before impact.

Her instincts ablaze with sensitivity, she stepped sideways, turned, and braced for the blow.

But it was too late.

The small coastal town of Saint-Pierre was a maze of back streets that encircled a small marina, which provided berthing for the wealthy to moor their yachts and enjoy the fine restaurants and bars. To one side of the marina was a small fishing port where local fishermen could unload their catch to sell in the famous Saint-Pierre fish market. The rush of traffic in comparison to Harvey's sleepy village was enough for Harvey to consider turning back.

But there was nowhere for him to go.

An image of the smouldering ruins of his house clung to the forefront of his mind and a familiar feeling stirred inside him, in the very pit of his stomach.

He pulled over beside a café where a few locals enjoyed coffee and cigarettes at small tables placed in a long row on the footpath. He raised his visor and caught the attention of an old man.

"Hospital?" he said, and shrugged, the international gesture for not knowing.

"Anglais?" said the old man. Then he mumbled some French with accompanying hand signs to indicate that Harvey should turn right, and shouldn't ask any more questions.

Harvey nodded his thanks, pulled his visor down and entered the traffic. A set of lights had created a small tailback, but Harvey weaved through the cars then sped to the front of the queue on the wrong side of the street. Seeing a gap in the traffic, he kicked down into second gear and tore up the road.

Harvey slowed for a junction and his heart sank.

In the traffic on the opposite side of the road, two men stared at him from inside a black SUV.

It jumped into life as the driver pulled a U-turn. The junction ahead was blocked with cars so Harvey made his way along the outside on the wrong side of the road. The SUV driver followed, spanning the centre line and causing the oncoming cars to swerve out of its way.

They were closing in fast when Harvey ducked into the traffic, weaving at a crawl between the cars waiting for the lights to change.

The SUV driver's window opened and a spray of automatic fire whistled through the air above Harvey's head. He opened the throttle, revving the engine loudly. With cars either side of him just inches from his hands on the handlebars, he forged a path between the two lines of traffic.

The SUV followed on the opposite side of the road, creating havoc as cars swerved and honked their horns. The man with the gun continued to lay down fire in bursts of three, stopping only to change magazines when needed. At the front of the queue of traffic was a busy junction with the marina on Harvey's left and another turn on the right. The SUV drew up level with him. The automatic fire stopped; another magazine change.

Harvey chanced his luck. He tore across the front of the SUV into the right turn and merged with the stream of oncoming traffic. Wheels spun as the SUV followed. A glance in Harvey's mirror showed the huge SUV towering above the small European cars, swerving between them like a raging bull.

A maze of narrow alleyways cut through the rows of small, white-washed houses. Harvey dropped his knee, leaned into the turn, and accelerated into an alley. He put as much distance as he could between his bike and the SUV. But they followed. The driver sent the car sideways to make the turn. Then it straightened and stormed into the alley behind Harvey, knocking over garbage bins, smashing through anything that stood in its way, and leaving a trail of destruction in its wake.

Sirens sounded close by. As Harvey burst from the alleyway, across a road, and into the next alley, he caught the flash off blue light on the road parallel to his right. He slowed. At a cross junction of alleyways, he took the next left. It was a dead end.

Behind him, the roar of the SUV's engine grew louder.

Around him, the whine of police cars grew closer.

With high walls to his left and right and a chain link fence in front of him, Harvey turned the bike, dropped one leg to the ground and pulled the handgun from his waist.

The SUV skidded to a halt, blocking Harvey's exit.

The first shot Harvey let off hit the front left tyre. The second smashed the side window. And as the passenger fought to change magazines, Harvey planted the third shot into his neck. The driver crunched the car into reverse and spun the wheels, leaving a trail of thick tyre smoke. Dogs barked, disturbed by the action, and a German Shepherd jumped at the fence to Harvey's left, teeth bared. It snarled at Harvey, barked once, and then offered a low growl that diminished along with its anger. The dog returned to all fours then sat on its haunches and cocked its head, waiting for Harvey to respond.

Instead, Harvey kicked the bike into first. As the road ahead cleared of tyre smoke, he burst through, firing at the car as he passed. But despite the punctured tyre, the driver gave chase. The SUV filled Harvey's side mirror, slewing from side to side and filling the alleyway with its mass.

The exit to the road was ahead. But as Harvey kicked down into third to speed across into the next alleyway, two police cars skidded to a stop and blocked the exit. With the SUV picking up speed behind him and the road ahead jammed, Harvey was trapped.

He slowed then stopped twenty yards from the police. He heard the SUV slow behind him as the bare alloy rim scraped against the concrete track.

Behind him, a car door opened and a heavy boot stepped down from the SUV. But Harvey kept his eyes on the police ahead who were climbing from two small Peugeots, guns in hands.

Scenarios played out in Harvey's mind. The driver of the SUV had an automatic weapon, drove as if he'd been trained to drive, and wore military issue boots just like the intruder, Freddie. The two policemen each had a handgun, were overweight, and couldn't hit the side of a bus if it was parked beside them.

"Stone," called the driver of the SUV. Harvey put the distance at thirty yards and recognised the accent as English. But he didn't turn. "You have something of ours. Let me have it and you can go."

Harvey didn't reply.

"Don't do anything stupid," said the driver.

His voice was nearer now, as if he was closing the gap.

Harvey revved the engine. As expected, the two policemen cowered behind their cars and re-aimed their weapons.

"Put the gun down," said the SUV driver, his voice even closer.

Harvey dropped the gun to the ground.

"That's it. Put your hands in the air. Nice and slow."

Harvey raised his hands then rolled his head to the left. He felt the click of his joints, and then did the same to the right. Taking a deep breath, he waited. His eyes gazed past the cops and he saw, in the distance, a single building taller than the rest of the town. The hospital.

The moment the man's hand grabbed Harvey's wrist, he sprang into action. Twisting the man's arm backwards with one hand, Harvey whipped his knife from his belt with the other and slashed across the man's gut.

He stepped back in shock at the speed of which Harvey had attacked him. One hand on his stomach held the two flaps of skin together as blood seeped out across his arm. The other raised the automatic rifle at Harvey. The man's mouth was open, aghast at the wound. The rifle began to shake and even as he dropped to one knee, he fought his trembling hand, trying to squeeze the trigger. He fell forward onto his face and a three-round burst fire dotted the two police cars, sending the policemen diving to the ground for cover.

Harvey jumped back onto his bike, revved the engine once, kicked it into first, and shot into the next alley, leaving the two policemen cowering on the ground and the man in black fighting for his life.

"The last syringe, if you will, Doctor Farrow," said Kane, as he watched the doctor pacing the room.

The doctor ignored his request. He lifted one of the two gurneys into the air and slammed it into the glass wall with little effect. Then he staggered backwards, drunk on adrenaline and fuelled by his own creation.

"Come now, Doctor. Just a little more medicine and it'll all be over," said Kane.

Through the speakers built into the control panel, the raspy breathing of Doctor Farrow could be heard as the oxygen ran low. The doctor staggered forward then dropped to his knees, one hand clutching his throat, the other feeling the thick, blue vein protruding from the side of his head.

"I need air," said Farrow.

"And I need results, Doctor Farrow," said Kane, his tone sharp and his impatience evident. "The last syringe, Doctor Farrow. Then I'll give you all the air you want."

A shaky hand reached onto the stainless steel tray and felt for the last remaining syringe.

"That-a-boy, Doctor Farrow," said Kane. He dropped his feet from the control panel and sat forward with interest.

But the doctor's shaking hand failed to grasp the syringe. His fingers fumbled and the syringe fell to the floor, where, on his hands and knees, the doctor searched for it. He moved his head from side to side as if only the very centre of his vision provided the clarity he needed to see; his peripheral was a mass of blur.

"A little to the left, Doctor." Kane watched as Farrow found the syringe and worked his elbow to produce a vein. "There you go. Nice and slow."

With a practiced hand, the doctor arranged the syringe. He searched for Kane through the window, but his eyes, blackened and dilated by the drug, failed to focus on anything beyond the sheen of the glass.

"In it goes," said Kane, like he was convincing a child to eat the last of his greens.

But the doctor, panting for breath, sat with his knees splayed, all willingness to live gone from his eyes. Shifting the air control slider forward a fraction of an inch, Kane teased the doctor with a blast of cool air then pulled it back and heard the fans slow to a stop.

"That's all for now," said Kane. Then he turned to the doorway as Jones stepped into view. "You're just in time for the show."

Jones glanced into the control room. He saw the upturned

gurneys and the suffocating doctor poised with the syringe held above his arm.

"It's time, Farrow," said Kane, and he released the MIC button.

"It's time for what?" asked Jones.

"You'll see," replied Kane, without removing his eyes from the doctor. Farrow touched the needle to his skin and pushed the tip onto his vein, making a new hole beside four others.

"Squeeze," Kane whispered. "Show me what you've got, Doctor Farrow."

In just a few seconds, the plunger reached the bottom of the chamber. Weakened by the lack of oxygen and control over his body, Farrow fumbled to pull the needle out.

"How many?" asked Jones.

"That was number five," said Kane, who continued to watch as the doctor got to his feet.

"What's happening to him?" asked Jones, wide-eyed.

The doctor staggered to his feet with his mouth open and pointed to the vents high in the walls.

"There's an energy inside him like you never thought possible, Jones," said Kane. "He's had so much of the proto-type that he no longer needs adrenaline to trigger its effects. Communication to his mind from his limbs and organs are numbed. He'll feel no pain. He's lost control of his senses, including the ability to talk, hear, smell and, as far as I can tell, see."

"He looks drunk," said Jones.

"It's similar, Jones. Right now, the drug is searching for any usable energy inside his body. His internal organs are being eaten and his blood is thick with the most intoxicating drug known to mankind."

"Adrenaline?" said Jones.

"That's right. Let's give him some air, shall we?" Kane slid the slider forward to full. Above him, the fans kicked into life and the doctor raised his arms in welcome at the cool breeze.

"Tell me about the girl, Jones," said Kane. "Are you sure she's dead?"

"Like I told you over the radio, she was hit by a bus. I stayed until the ambulance took her away."

"And do we have a problem?" asked Kane.

"No," said Jones, captivated by the doctor, who was shuffling across the floor towards the control room window. "No, she won't be a problem anymore. I radioed Sierra team to pay the hospital a visit to make sure she doesn't get a second wind."

"I was referring to the missing vial."

Jones was silent. He stammered then quietened once more.

"Jones?" said Kane. "Where is the vial?"

"Gone."

Kane turned to face his number two.

"Gone? How can it be gone?"

"She said she hid it somewhere."

A loud bang against the glass caught both men's attention.

"Where did she hide it, Jones?" said Kane, eying Farrow.

Another bang. The doctor peered into the control room. His dark eyes searched the room, and his tongue hung from his open mouth, dry and lifeless. He slammed his forehead into the window. Then he stared at Kane with his eyes an inch from the reinforced glass.

"She said she gave it to some guy for safekeeping."

Another bang on the glass. A web of angry, red arteries had begun to form on the doctor's forehead.

"And did you get this man's name?" asked Kane, as the doctor prepared for another attack.

"No. But Foxtrot destroyed his house as you requested,"

said Jones, hoping the positive news would counter the negative.

"And?" said Kane, more interested in Farrow's behaviour.

"He searched the house for the vial. Found nothing."

"I'm guessing there's more?"

"The man is Harvey Stone," said Jones. "Foxtrot found some ID. He's just some local guy."

Farrow's third head-butt split skin. A spatter of blood remained on the glass as the doctor pulled away.

"Good. Make sure Foxtrot one is rewarded for his work. At least someone is switched on."

"Not possible, I'm afraid, sir," said Jones.

Kane's head remained forward, but his eyes swivelled to find Jones taking a step back.

"Stone killed him, sir."

"Find him," said Kane. "Find him and kill him."

8

NO QUARTER

A SURGE OF ACID BILE RUSHED FROM GABRIELLA'S STOMACH to her tongue; she rolled onto her side, opened her mouth and let it fall to the floor.

The familiar warm tingle in her fingertips ran up her arms like the last reach of the incoming tide. A pulse of blood rushed through her body, leaving her pale skin prickling as she sucked in a lungful of air and rolled onto her back. A throb inside her head kept time with her heart, which began to increase as consciousness crept over her.

Behind her eyelids, a bright light shone. It was enough for her to keep her eyes closed and let the pounding throb acclimatise. She lay back, controlling her breathing, as images from before unconsciousness flashed across her mind.

The trees.

The man.

She gasped when she thought of the man she'd killed, and her hands flexed in response.

Then that voice.

Jones.

The road, the horn and then…

She sat up as her last memory came back and she gasped for breath.

The bus.

But there was no pain.

She eyed her surroundings and found that she was sitting on a gurney in a white room. The clothes she'd been given by Harvey Stone were piled on a small chair to one side.

"No," she said. "I can't be back here again."

Darkness crept to the edges of her vision, a hint at the sickness that was to follow.

Voices in the hallway were muffled by the door but clear in Gabriella's mind as her enhanced senses focused.

Two men.

Wearing boots.

Not doctors.

She pulled the sheet from her body and slid her legs off the bed. An angry, purple bruise ran from her chest to her thighs, six inches wide with yellow around the edges.

An image of the bus moments before it had hit her flashed across her mind. As if to confirm her memory, a dull throb pulsed once in the centre of the bruise.

There was no pain as her feet touched the linoleum floor, only trepidation.

The voices grew louder. As Gabriella pulled on her clothes, the crackle of a two-way radio confirmed her suspicion. She snatched back the curtain that surrounded her bed and found a window with a view of the Mediterranean, a road, and a few small buildings. She counted the five floors to the ground but couldn't remember the lab being so high.

Or the bed having curtains.

A touch of the door handle teased her heightened senses in time for her to launch a chair at her visitors, which the first man took square in the face. He stumbled back as Gabriella tried to smash the window.

But it was stuck.

The second man barged into the room, stepping over his friend, and pointed his handgun. He raised the radio to his mouth, keeping the gun on Gabriella.

"Charlie-two, this is Sierra-one. Asset has been located. She has a pulse."

He stared at Gabriella, keeping his distance as if she was some kind of wild animal. The radio crackled into life.

"Sierra-one, this is Charlie-two. Good work. Terminate the asset."

He smiled at Gabriella.

"Copy that, Charlie-two," said the man into the radio. "With pleasure."

Three sidesteps was all it took for Gabriella to close the gap. She reached up, twisted the handgun, and two shots found the white plastered wall. Using her momentum, she planted her shoulder into the man's stomach, driving forward until they both slammed into the wall.

But the move hadn't earned her any time. The man returned the attack with a left hook to Gabriella's face while his gun was pinned to the wall above his head. The blow rocked Gabriella, but no pain found its way to her brain. Instead, she responded with a head-butt that flattened the man's nose. A second blow cracked his eye socket. But before she could deliver the third, the first man rose beside her and slammed the butt of his pistol into her face.

The shock knocked her across the bed, where she rolled and hit the floor. She slid beneath the curtains, searching for a weapon. But the two men moved fast. They snatched back the curtains and tore them from the rails then closed in either side of the gurney. One man on the right. One man on the left.

In Gabriella's heightened mind, possibilities flashed by. Take the bigger man on the right and escape through the door. Take the smaller man on the left, kill him fast, and then deal with the bigger man one-on-one.

She stepped toward the window, the sunlight blinding her. But as her vision returned, a shape appeared behind the two men that changed everything.

The hospital was a small five-story building painted white to match the surrounding neighbourhood of whitewashed houses and shops. A single entrance for ambulances was at the end of the short curved driveway. In a spot marked for emergencies only was a black SUV identical to the one Harvey had seen outside the police station and in the alleyway.

Harvey parked his bike on the pavement and entered the building. The nurse behind the reception glanced up at him, noticed the blood on his leg and the dust on his jacket, and tried to catch his attention. But seeing the sign above her head that read *traumatisme* with a number five in a small blue circle beside it, he moved toward the two small elevators without needing her help. He stepped inside as the doors were closing, just catching sight of the security guard who had been summoned by the receptionist.

The doors opened with a weak ping. One day a long time ago, it may have been loud and sustained but had tired from years of relentless use. Harvey stepped out into the corridor. He glanced left and right. To his right was a nurse's station. To his left were a few small, private rooms. Harvey turned left, peering into each one as he passed. Each of the doors were closed except one at the end of the corridor. Behind it were the unmistakable sounds of a struggle taking place.

Harvey stepped into the doorway.

Two men had trapped Gabriella, each one approaching from either side of the hospital bed, moving with caution and closing her in against the window. Collecting a fire extinguisher from the wall in the hallway, and with no hesitation, Harvey slammed it into the back of the larger man's head. He fell to the floor with ease. The smaller man to Harvey's right stepped back to raise his weapon. But Harvey threw the fire extinguisher at his head then shoved the bed toward him, crushing him against the wall.

"Shut the door," said Harvey to Gabriella, who jumped into action. "Lock it."

A single twist of the gun disarmed the man and broke his index finger. Harvey released the magazine onto the floor and held the weapon out for Gabriella, who took it without question.

Men began to bang on the door and shout in French. But Harvey ignored them. He dragged the bed out of the way and hoisted the smaller man to his feet. The man wore the same uniform as the intruder at Harvey's house and the man in the alley: a simple black shirt with epaulettes, black cargo pants and black military boots.

Harvey slammed the man's head into the wall.

"Cassius Kane," said Harvey. "Where can I find him?"

But the man said nothing. He stared at the floor as if he hadn't heard the question.

Three more times Harvey slammed the back of his head into the wall.

"Kane," he said. "Tell me where I can find him."

"You won't find him," said the man.

His eyes were squeezed shut and his hands reached up to hold the back of his head. But Harvey caught hold of his right hand, twisted his wrist and pushed it over the man's head until he felt the crunch of his shoulder joint dislocating, followed by a satisfying scream of confirmation.

The men outside began to force the door.

"They're going to break through," said Gabriella. "Merde."

"Block the door," said Harvey.

"But we will be trapped."

"We'll use the window. Just block the door."

"The window is locked. I tried it already," said Gabriella, as she pushed the bed to the door and tucked the metal frame beneath the handle.

Harvey grabbed the man by his collar.

"This is your last chance. Where can I find Kane?"

The man smiled up at him, dazed from the blows to the back of his head. Then he spat in Harvey's face. But his laugh soon faded as Harvey lifted him from the floor, turned, then launched him head-first through the fifth-floor window.

The window shattered and shards of glass rained down to the ground below.

"Are you crazy? We are five floors up, Monsieur Stone," said Gabriella, leaning against the bed with all her weight as the men outside tried to force their way into the room.

Harvey peered down at the ground below. The man's body lay spread-eagled on the concrete. A pool of red was forming by his head. A woman screamed and two nurses ran to his aid. To Harvey's right, along the outside of the building, there was a narrow ledge in the brickwork, level with the bottom of the window frame, and another level with the top.

He ducked back inside the room.

"Are you coming or staying?" he asked.

"What?" said Gabriella, eying the door and then Harvey, who stood with his foot on the window ledge ready to climb through it. "Why are you doing this? Why are you helping me?"

"The man that kidnapped you, what was his name?"

"Cassius Kane," replied Gabriella.

"Can you take me to him?"

The effort against the outside of the door increased, and the entire frame began to shift in the wall as a fire axe attacked the door.

The radio in Harvey's pocket, which he had stolen from Freddie, crackled into life once more. So did the radio on the belt of the large man who'd received the fire extinguisher in his face. But this time, instead of the tinny voice with the London accent, it was a well-spoken man, mature and with an air of authority.

"Sierra-one, come back," said the voice.

Harvey looked across at Gabriella, who held the bed against the door as the axe broke through the wood. Two security guards peered through the splintered hole. Harvey pulled the radio from his pocket.

"Sierra-one, come back. This is Charlie-one."

"Is this Cassius Kane?" said Harvey, then he released the push-to-talk button and waited for the response. He remained calm and composed despite Gabriella's frantic efforts to hold the door.

"You must be Harvey Stone," said Kane after a pause. "You're becoming quite a nuisance, Mr Stone."

"Ditto," said Harvey.

"You have something that belongs to me."

Harvey didn't reply. He looked up at Gabriella, who said nothing but stared wide-eyed at the radio.

"Why don't you bring me what's mine and you can go about your life?"

Harvey stared at the girl, who pleaded with her eyes and shook her head.

"Do you know where to find him?" asked Harvey.

Gabriella nodded.

A crowd was gathering around the body on the ground outside and the door splintered again as the axe came through once more, widening the hole as two more men fought to get into the room.

But Harvey remained calm, considering his options.

"You're making a big mistake, Mr Stone," said Kane. "You don't know who you're dealing with here. Bring me what's mine and you walk. Enough blood has been shed."

Harvey depressed the button on the radio, silencing the static.

"Negative, Kane," said Harvey. "It's you who doesn't know who you're dealing with. You just destroyed everything I own. I'm coming for you, and I won't stop until I kill you."

"Who is this man?" asked Kane, and he threw the radio across the room. "He's clearly not just some local guy."

"He's taken down five of my men," said Jones, as Doctor Farrow planted his head into the glass. Blood leaked from several wounds on his forehead, and he gazed like an old drunk through the window at Kane and Jones. "Local police won't help anymore. They say it's too hard to explain a murder in the town in broad daylight. If there's more trouble, they'll be forced to get involved and make arrests."

"Cowards. They're just afraid because the prime minister is on his way. Any other day of the year and they'd be lining their corrupt pockets."

"We're on our own, sir," said Jones. "And either this guy has help, or he's-"

"He's what?" snapped Kane.

"I don't know. Ex-military? Special forces?"

"Jones, do I need to remind you that you have a whole

team of ex-special forces men and this guy is picking us off like they're old grannies."

"I'm aware of my team's capabilities, sir," said Jones.

"But you're not aware of *his* capabilities. Know your enemy, Jones. The first rule of war."

"We can't find anything on him, sir," said Jones. "We've checked the police databases. We even had the local police check Interpol."

"Military?" said Kane.

"Nothing, sir. He doesn't exist."

"So who killed five of your men?" said Kane. "Who is it that has my vial? I want him dead, whoever this Stone is. I want his head on a stick and I want my vial back."

As if in response to Kane's mention of the vial, the doctor head-butted the partition once more, his breath fogging the bloodied glass.

"We're doing everything we can, sir. I've got all teams out looking for him."

"All teams? And what happens if he chews through those like he has the rest?"

Jones remained silent, unable to find a suitable answer.

"When the prime minister drives into Saint-Pierre, I want all bases covered. If we can pull this mission off, we'll be set for life. We'll have every government on the planet bidding for our services."

"I'll pull three teams, sir," said Jones. "Alpha team, Bravo team and Tango team. Alpha team will cover the entrance to the town. Bravo team will monitor the ambush site. Tango team will be the eyes in the sky in the tower."

"You're missing the point," said Kane. "Without the vial, even if we do pull this off, we have nothing to make us stand out from the crowd. We'll just be another rogue team of hired guns, and if Stone carries on the way he is, we won't even be a team. It'll be you and I standing there with our dicks in our hands begging for work."

"We don't need the drug, sir. I'm sure we can pull this off."

"Of course we can pull it off, Jones. It's not exactly a difficult mission. But I offered the men a future. I offered them a chance to clear their names, a chance at success and honour. That's what soldiers fight for, Jones. Honour. And in return for honour, they offer loyalty. That's how it works, Jones. That's how the system has functioned since the Romans and it's no different now."

"Loyalty isn't a question, sir. Every one of my men is loyal to a tee."

"Apart from the ones that Stone has hit already?"

Jones said nothing in response. Instead, he cocked his head to one side. Kane's lip curled at the mannerism he had always detested.

"Presuming we have enough men to pull off the mission, presuming we are successful, and presuming we get the vial back then we might just have a future, Jones. We might be able to offer the men a taste of honour. And they might, in return, offer us prolonged loyalty. Presuming the stars align and the heavens shine down on us, we might just get another job. And if I'm right, Jones, which I often am, we'll take that vial, and we'll make enough of it to last a lifetime. Our men will be unstoppable and everyone will be calling us. And you know what that means?"

"Money?"

"Blank cheques, Jones," said Kane. "That's when we get to write ourselves a blank cheque. What's that, Mr President? You're having trouble with the Columbians and their drug enterprise? Don't you worry. We'll take care of it. Oh, hello, Mr Minister of Defence. You need a village taken out in deepest, darkest Afghanistan and you can't send your boys in because you don't have one-hundred-percent proof it's full of terrorists? Don't worry. Our boys will take care of it for you. The same will happen with the United Kingdom, that very same country that trained us and nurtured us from young boys into the men we are now. The same country that took the best years of our lives, and took the best we had to give, then tossed us aside with shame after one simple mistake. You watch, Jones. If we can pull this off, you watch those bastards come crawling when they can't launch an attack because of some bullshit peace deal they made fifty years ago. When they're so tied up in the politics they can't see the wood for the trees, we'll be the ones they come to, Jones. We'll be the ones they call for help. And who knows? When that time comes, I might even offer them a free deal. A coupon, if you like. We'll go in and sort out their mess. We'll clear up what they can't. In return, we'll have our dirty, dishonourable discharges relinquished. Every one of your men will walk the streets with his head held high, Jones. Can you imagine that? Imagine the honour. Imagine the loyalty."

"It's a dream I have every day, sir," said Jones.

"Good," said Kane. "You keep dreaming of it. But let me tell you something. If you and your boys don't get me that vial, and if you and your boys don't pull this mission off tomorrow morning, it'll only be a dream. Nothing more. We'll all be downtrodden, disgraced scum for the rest of our lives."

"Understood, sir," said Jones.

"Stand to attention when I'm talking to you, Jones."

Snapping into life, Jones' right leg came up, bending at ninety degrees. His right boot stamped down beside the left. His chest stood out with pride. His back held ramrod straight and his arms fixed to his sides with his thumbs pointing down the seams of his pants.

"Do you understand the mission, soldier?" said Kane.

"Yes, sir," barked Jones.

"What are your primary objectives?"

"Find the missing vial, sir, and complete the mission with no fatalities."

Kane nodded. He stood from his chair, face to face with Jones, their eyes aligned.

"And how do you plan on achieving this, soldier?" said Kane.

"Destroy Harvey Stone, sir."

9

US AND THEM

"You're coming with me," said Harvey, leaning in through the window. "Pass me the gun."

Gabriella followed his instruction and handed him the dead soldier's gun. Harvey took it. As Gabriella climbed up through the window and dared a glance down, he opened fire on the door.

"What are you doing?" said Gabriella, ducking out of the way.

"Buying us time," said Harvey.

"Well, now what?" said Gabriella. "I'm guessing you have a plan?"

Harvey looked right along the tiny ledge then back at Gabriella.

"This is all I've got," replied Harvey. "Don't look down."

The words triggered a rush of blood to her head. Gabriella felt the warm tingle of SFS strengthening her fingertips.

Harvey waited, half in and half out of the window, staring at her when she opened her eyes.

"What are you waiting for, Monsieur Stone?" she asked.

That seemed to be all the encouragement Harvey needed. He edged along the tiny ledge to the corner of the building. Gabriella followed. Her foot stepped off the window sill and onto the narrow ledge just as the door crashed open inside the room. Two men in black uniforms burst through the broken window and peered out in disbelief. One of the men raised his weapon; the shot found the bare concrete wall as Gabriella slipped around the corner.

A steel fire escape ladder stood fixed to the building. The narrow ledge finished eight feet short of it.

"We have to jump," said Harvey, his fingers gripping just an inch of brickwork. The toes of his boots were turned sideways for maximum support.

"You first," said Gabriella, feeling another surge of energy, clarity and focus. It was as if only the ledge and the jump existed. The shouts and calls from the people on the ground were held at bay by her mind and drowned out by SFS.

With almost no hesitation, Harvey leapt from the ledge with his arms stretched out. His fingers just managed to grab onto a handrail while the rest of his body slammed into the steel framework. He slipped down, and just as Gabriella thought he would fall, he caught himself.

A thick drool of sticky blood leaked from a gash in his leg.

"Are you okay?" called Gabriella, as Harvey pulled himself onto the steel platform. He rolled to his feet and prepared to help her, his face masking his certain pain.

Gabriella pushed off with her right foot. Her left leg extended. Her foot found the framework and her hands clamped onto the handrail. She swung once to allow her momentum to disperse. Then, on the return swing, she hoisted herself over the handrail and landed beside Harvey who was crouched with his arm ready to catch her.

"Let's go," she replied, and stepped past him to the ladder.

A single gunshot rang out. The bullet pinged off the steel

framework above. A large man in a black uniform was leaning out of a fourth-floor window, gun poised to fire again.

Gabriella slid down the ladder with her feet and hands on the sides of the rails. Harvey dropped to one knee, aimed and fired, sending the man back inside.

Matching his speed, Gabriella landed on each landing as Harvey landed on the one above her. By the time she reached the ground, a crowd had gathered to watch the spectacle. Mobile phones were recording the dramatic video. Harvey dropped down beside her, limped, grunted, and dropped to the ground, clutching his wounded leg.

"We need to get you out of here," said Gabriella.

"You need to show me where to find Kane," he replied.

"But your leg. You need to get it looked at."

Harvey didn't reply. He stood, took a breath, and searched around him at the faces of the crowds that were snapping shots as if they were celebrities. He grabbed Gabriella's hand and made his way to the front of the hospital, barging through the crowd. Gabriella followed, hiding her face from the phones. This time, Harvey didn't hand her a helmet. Nor did he give her any instructions. He started the engine, waited for Gabriella to climb onto the bike, then roared off across the manicured lawn into the heavy traffic.

The black SUV swung onto the main road behind them as the driver fought to hold the turn with all four tyres screeching. He locked onto Gabriella and Harvey, and accelerated hard.

Gabriella tapped Harvey on the shoulder and leaned into his ear.

"They're behind us," she called.

Harvey glanced into his mirror, saw the SUV approaching, and then turned suddenly into a side street away from the marina and up a small hill. The SUV followed with speed. Harvey slowed the bike until the SUV was just a few seconds away then jammed on the rear brake, sliding the bike around to face the car head on.

He flicked up his visor, raised his weapon and aimed, finding the accelerating SUV along the short length of the handgun.

The driver's head became clear through the windshield.

Still, the SUV accelerated towards them, now only one hundred yards away.

"Monsieur Stone," said Gabriella.

Her weight shifted as if she was preparing to jump from the bike.

Harvey fingered the trigger, letting the steel bed into the first crevice of his index finger.

"*Monsieur Stone*," said Gabriella once more, as the vehicle closed in at forty yards with no intention of avoiding them.

Harvey squeezed the trigger.

One shot killed the driver.

The SUV turned, slammed into the line of parked cars and flipped. All four wheels left the ground and the huge car completed a full roll before it crashed down on its roof, embedding its front end into the windshield of a parked van. Shopkeepers emerged from their doorways and passers-by fled to spectate from a safe distance.

The carnage came to a stop.

Broken glass fell to the tarmac road.

A hand appeared through the gap where the windscreen had been.

The passenger of the SUV crawled from the broken window and fell to the ground in a heap among the glass. His face was a bloodied mess. Harvey kicked down the bike stand and dismounted. He limped over to the man, gun in hand and oblivious to the spectators or the approaching sirens.

Gabriella remained on the bike. She watched as Harvey stood over the man on the ground.

"No, Monsieur Stone," she called.

But it was too late.

Harvey raised his gun. Aimed. Pulled the trigger.

Harvey returned to the bike and shoved the gun into his waistband. "You and I need to talk." He stood in front of Gabriella with his hands on his hips. "What does Kane want with you?"

"Who knows?" said Gabriella with a shrug. But she knew it was not convincing. "Are you going after him?" she asked, in an effort to steer him away from the truth.

"He destroyed everything I own," said Harvey, then he climbed onto the bike.

"I can help," said Gabriella.

"And why would you do that?" said Harvey, kicking the bike stand back up.

Gabriella hesitated, but Harvey waited for her response.

"He's planning to kill the prime minister."

Sirens in all directions wailed across the small town, growing louder as the net closed in on Harvey and Gabriella.

"It's Kane," said Gabriella, "he's paid the police off."

"We need to go."

Harvey climbed onto the bike as a police car came screeching into the road from the marina. As Gabriella slid on behind him, he kicked into first gear, opened the throttle and spun the rear wheel, holding the front brake until the bike had turned a full one hundred and eighty degrees to head out of the town. Open-mouthed onlookers were buried in the tyre smoke, and only the shrill whistle of the sirens cut through the roar of Harvey's bike.

They breached a small hill at the edge of town, only to find two police Peugeots waiting for them and parked in a Vshape blocking the road ahead. With the police car behind them approaching fast, Harvey tore into an alleyway at full speed. Both sides, the backs of houses opened up into small courtyards, and ahead, tall pines marked the edge of the town and the start of the forest.

Bursting from one alleyway without stopping, they sped across the road and into another. Gabriella tapped Harvey on the shoulder and leaned into him.

"They are behind us, Monsieur Stone. Two police cars and another big black car. What should I do?"

"Hold on tight," said Harvey, as they approached the end of the last alleyway.

He slowed the bike to make the turn at the end onto the road then opened the throttle and headed back towards the town.

"Are we trapped?" said Gabriella.

Harvey didn't reply.

He cut through the traffic on the marina road, and used the opposite lane to put some distance between him and the men in black. The wind rushed past, stinging his eyes, and the biting cold gnawed at his hands. Still, the black SUV followed, bullying the oncoming traffic out of its way.

Harvey slowed once more, preparing to turn onto the road out of town after completing a full circle of Saint-Pierre. A large lorry nosed into view, turning toward Harvey's speeding bike.

The black SUV roared up behind them, its grill inches from Harvey's back wheel.

Harvey pulled his weapon from his belt and steered into the path of the lorry.

Seeing Harvey's maneuverer, the lorry driver pulled on the horn, the anger on his face clear even from two hundred yards away, and turned the steering wheel hard to avoid a collision.

The SUV nudged the back of the bike.

Harvey accelerated away at the last minute, aiming his gun with one hand as he passed the turning lorry, and firing a single shot into its off-side tyre.

The shift in weight along with the driver's hard turn sent the lorry leaning over. As Harvey braked hard to make the turn out of town, a quick glance in his mirror showed the toppling lorry and the SUV that buried itself into it. Speeding police Peugeots followed a few seconds later.

Once out of town, Harvey made for the forest, where he stopped the bike in a copse of trees atop the tallest hill for miles around. Behind them, at the foot of the hill, Saint-Pierre lay sprawled across the valley between the two surrounding mountains that met the sea. The noises of the sirens continued in the distance. But Harvey and Gabriella's escape had been successful.

"Tell me everything you know," said Harvey, as he checked the magazine in his Sig and found just one round remaining.

Stepping off the bike, he stumbled on his injured leg. He grimaced but held the pain inside.

"I have told you everything, Monsieur Stone," said Gabriella, eying his leg. "They kidnapped me, I escaped, and now they want me back."

With one smooth movement, Harvey caught her by the throat with his freezing hands, pulled her from the bike, and slammed her against a tree.

She stared at him in defiance until he plunged his knife into the bark beside her head.

"Don't take me for a fool, Gabriella," said Harvey.

With eyes wide open, she stared back at him. She was searching for something, buying time to think of a lie.

"Who is Kane?" said Harvey.

"He's a madman."

Harvey didn't reply.

"He is ex-military, British, I think. An officer. Or at least he acts like one."

"And his men?"

"They are all ex-military. All rogue. Shunned by the services with dishonourable discharges."

"What did they do?"

"I don't know. Something bad. In Afghanistan. It was covered up but they were discharged. Now they work for whoever offers the biggest paycheck."

"And they're planning to kill the French prime minister?" asked Harvey. "How do you know this?"

"I overheard," said Gabriella, shrugging.

"And how is Kane planning on killing the prime minister?" asked Harvey.

"Every year, the prime minister spends Christmas on his yacht with his family. It's his tradition."

"But he'll be guarded. That's not an easy mission."

"Cassius Kane is a criminal genius," said Gabriella. The words came from her mouth with a look of distaste. "As much as I hate to admit it."

"So how's he going to do it?" asked Harvey.

"He has developed a drug. He may only have a few men, but with the drug, they will be unstoppable. We have to stop them, Monsieur Stone."

Harvey released his grip a little, but still held her against the tree.

"That's why they wanted me," she continued. "They used me as one of the test subjects."

"A what?"

"A lab rat, Monsieur Stone," said Gabriella. She blinked away the tears. "They killed us one by one, testing the drug, adapting it a little, then testing again until it did exactly what they wanted it to do."

"And what *does* it do?" asked Harvey.

"It gives you superpowers," said Gabriella, her French accent thick and romantic with the idea.

Harvey didn't reply. He stared at her with disbelief.

"You don't believe me?" said Gabriella.

Harvey shook his head.

"How do you think I escaped from a high-security facility? How do you think I killed those men myself? Me? How do you think I survived being hit by a bus, Harvey? And how, god damn it, do you think I climbed out of that hospital with you?"

"The drug," said Harvey.

"Yes, Harvey. Have you ever felt the power of adrenaline? Have you ever felt its release into your blood stream and felt your power grow?"

"Often," said Harvey.

"Imagine if that adrenaline was amplified. Imagine if your body felt no pain. Imagine if your senses were heightened to an animal-like state."

"And Kane thinks he's going to take over the world?"

"No, Harvey, not the world. But he'll be unstoppable. Think of what a government could do with a drug like that. How much would they pay to have Kane's men do what a government is not allowed to do?"

"And that's why he wants you back?" said Harvey. "Because you know all his plans?"

"Well, yes and no. He wants the vial I stole," said Gabriella, offering a cunning smile. "His men will be more powerful than any men in any army. All communications between the muscles and the brain are blocked. Your body is far stronger than you know, Harvey Stone."

"A drug like that would be worth a fortune on the black market," said Harvey.

"In the right hands, a drug like that could stop many wars," said Gabriella. "But it's worth far more if only Kane's men have access to it."

"I can't be involved in all of that, Gabriella," said Harvey, and he released her from his grip. He stepped away and looked out over Saint-Pierre.

"Do you still want to kill him?" said Gabriella, her voice soft.

He felt her step up beside him and tracked her movements as she took his hand in her own, then lowered her head to kiss it.

"Where's the vial now?" asked Harvey.

A bead of sweat fell from Gabriella's brow onto Harvey's hand.

"I have hidden it," she replied.

Harvey removed his hand and stuffed it into his pocket.

"Hidden it where?" he asked.

"The safest place I know," said Gabriella. "But his men are still strong. He has a prototype."

"Kane took everything from me," said Harvey. "Drug or no drug, I'm going to kill him."

"Then I will help you," said Gabriella.

"I don't need help," said Harvey, relaxing his grip and stepping back from Gabriella. "Just tell me where to find him."

With both hands nursing her throat, Gabriella moved away from him and stopped at the edge of the hill, gazing across the valley at the town of Saint-Pierre.

She turned her head back to face Harvey.

"I will tell you where to find him," said Gabriella. "But first, you must help me stop the assassination."

Eight men stood in a single rank in the courtyard outside the research and development centre as the first drops of rain announced the onslaught of a winter storm. Each man had polished boots, shiny buckles and pressed black uniforms. In front of them, their leader, Sergeant Jones, stood with his hands crossed behind his back and his feet shoulder-width apart. He stared straight ahead. Not one man moved a muscle.

Kane watched them through the doors. His chest swelled with the pride of a father.

He pushed through the double doors, stepped out into the evening, and marched to the front with one arm swinging. He came to a halt in front of Jones, performed a right turn, and stared at his second in command.

"Squad, attention," called Jones.

The entire squad brought their right legs up to ninety degrees and then back down in unison to stand beside the left boot. Their arms moved to the side of their bodies, thumbs pointing down, chins up, and fearlessness etched onto each of their faces.

Jones raised a salute, his arm rigid and perfectly square with his body.

"Thank you, Sergeant," said Kane, returning the salute. "At ease."

"Stand at ease," barked Jones.

The squad reversed their move, returning to the more comfortable position with their hands behind their backs and feet shoulder-width apart.

Kane eyed his men, admiring their chiselled features, strong bodies and the determined looks on their faces. He turned to the left, moved his hands behind his back, and paced to the front of the squad. Then he stopped in front of the first man, the tallest and broadest of them all.

"Name," said Kane.

Without moving his eyes, the man stood to attention then replied in full volume, "Bravo-one, sir."

"Are you ready, Bravo-one?" said Kane, his voice low but clear.

"Yes, sir."

"Do you know what God has in store for you tonight?"

"Victory and honour, sir."

Kane cocked his head at the reply, surprised and impressed.

"Good. At ease," said Kane.

The soldier returned to the at-ease position.

Kane continued his inspection, eying the men's boots, belts and uniforms as he passed. He stopped at the last soldier in the front rank, a squat man who appeared as wide as he was tall.

"Name?"

The man stood to attention with precise movements, showing the result of years of training.

"Alpha-two, sir."

"Alpha-two," said Kane, "which way around did you enter this world? Feet first or sideways?"

"Head first, sir," replied Alpha-two.

"Is that right?"

"I wanted to see where I was going, sir," replied Alpha-two.

"That's always a good idea," said Kane. "Tell me, Alpha-two, who do you follow?"

"I follow you, sir."

"Just me?"

"And Sergeant Jones, sir."

"Who?"

"Charlie-two, sir."

"And what about your squad?"

"I don't follow them. I stand beside them, sir."

"Good answer," said Kane. "And God? Where does he stand?"

"He carries me, sir," said Alpha-two. He allowed himself a smile, but then corrected himself.

Kane nodded. "At ease, Alpha-two."

The soldier returned to the at-ease position.

Kane strode straight-legged to the front of the squad, letting his heels click on the concrete with each step. He stopped, eyed Jones, and then stood silent for a while; it was a method of finding weakness in the squad. Uncertainty caused the weakest of men to shuffle, a natural movement he'd picked up many years before his own dishonourable discharge.

When he spoke, he projected his voice with authority. It was loud enough to be heard, clear enough to be understood, but quiet enough to ensure that each man strived to hear him.

"I have never been so proud," began Kane. "I have served in Afghanistan, Europe, and all over our Queen's empire, and never before have I rested my eyes on such capable men with such strength and determination."

Each man remained still, their eyes facing forward, accepting the compliment in silence.

"You all know what we have to do tomorrow morning. You all know the dangers. In eight hours from now, the prime minister of France will arrive here in Saint-Pierre. All hell will break loose. You *will* remain calm. You will *not* stand down. We will be *victorious*. Is that understood?"

"Yes, sir," said the squad in unison. Their voices echoed off the walls of the courtyard then faded as each man waited for Kane to resume his speech.

"Some of you may not survive. I wish I could sugar-coat it. But it's a fact. You'll be up against some of the most patriotic, determined and ruthless individuals you ever came across. But that's what they are: individuals. They're not an army.

They're not like you. They don't have your training, your strength, and they don't have *this*."

Kane produced a single vial of prototype SFS and held it up for all to see.

"For six months, you've all been guarding this place, and for good reason. What I have in my hand will transform you. You think you're strong now? You think you're ruthless? Hard? Unstoppable?" Kane continued to hold the vial of red liquid high in the air, and met the eyes of each man as they stared at his hand. "No. You're wrong. But once you're charged with this, once this chemical finds its way into your blood, and the rush of battle hits you, nothing will stop you. I know the feeling a man gets when he puts his life on the line, as do all of you, when adrenaline takes over and you're so fired up you charge into battle screaming the Lord's name."

He paused to make sure he was holding their attention.

"This little vial is just a prototype. We have a stronger, more potent version. But even this tiny vial contains enough SFS to fire that adrenaline into action. It's just like flicking a switch. Each one of you will have the strength of ten men. Only then will you be unstoppable. Only then will you be the men you've been striving to be. When we win this battle, your names will go down in history. Not for the so-called crimes that we once committed, not for the infidelities that tarnished us and led us into the shadows, but for the honour you all deserve."

He paused once more to admire the looks on each of their faces: confidence, bravery, loyalty and trust.

"Tonight, gentlemen, you are Kane's Army. Who are you?"

"Kane's Army, sir," they replied, louder than before.

"Again?"

"Kane's Army, sir."

"And what do we want?"

"Victory, sir."

"Good," said Kane, allowing the noise to settle. He stood once more in front of Jones, coming to attention by bringing his right leg up and then stepping down beside his left.

"Squad, attention," called Jones, and the squad followed suit, their heels clicking on the concrete with unified perfection.

"Tonight, gentlemen, we have strength on our side. We have cunning. And we have God carrying us on our path to victory."

He met Alpha-two's eyes as the words left his mouth.

"Tonight, gentlemen," Kane continued, passing his gaze across his men, "we make history."

10

WHEN THE LEVEE BREAKS

"TAKE OFF YOUR PANTS. YOU ARE NO USE TO ANYONE WITH your leg like that," said Gabriella.

"I'll be fine," said Harvey. "I've had worse."

"Harvey Stone, do not take me for some kind of feeble, little girl. Tonight we will face Kane's Army and you are losing blood faster than your body can create it. Take your pants off and lie down on the ground."

Harvey didn't reply.

"That's an order, Monsieur Stone."

"I don't do so good with orders."

"So I gather," said Gabriella. "I don't do so good with partners who are bleeding to death. If you want to know how to find Kane, lie down and let me look at your leg."

Harvey dropped to the ground and peeled his cargo pants away from his thigh. The dried blood had stuck to his skin and the movement opened the wound further as he pulled the material free.

"There's water in the panniers," said Harvey, gesturing at the two boxes either side of the bike's rear wheel.

Gabriella fetched the bottles of water then slapped Harvey's hand away from his leg.

"Lie back," she said. "This will sting a little."

She ran her fingers around the five-inch wound on Harvey's thigh, nodding when she saw that the mouth-shaped ends had begun to heal. Her practiced eye confirmed no sign of infection. So, using her slender fingers to hold the wound open, she washed the cut with the cool water. Beneath her hands, Harvey's body tensed when the water splashed onto his pink flesh then eased as his body grew accustomed to the pain.

"How you doing up there?" she asked, as she gave the wound another careful check.

Harvey didn't reply.

"Give me your knife," said Gabriella.

Harvey's head raised from the ground, a questioning look on his face.

But Gabriella didn't respond to his lack of trust. She held out her hand.

"Knife."

With reluctance, Harvey pulled his knife from the sheave on his belt. He caught her eye, communicating some kind of warning, then spun the blade and offered her the weapon handle first.

Quick as a flash, and before Harvey could complain, Gabriella grabbed a handful of his t-shirt and cut a long strip from the hem. She was halfway through the cut when she met Harvey's eyes once more. This time, he offered the nearest she would get to an apology for not trusting her.

"You need to raise your leg," said Gabriella. "On three, you're going to rest your leg on mine. Don't bend it. I don't want the bleeding to start. Are you ready?"

Harvey blinked but didn't respond.

"One," said Gabriella. Then she lifted his leg onto hers before he had the chance to tense his muscle.

"Where did you learn to count?" asked Harvey.

"At military school."

"You were in the military?"

"I was a medic," said Gabriella, remembering the times she had used the *count to three* trick on other patients.

"Why did you leave?" asked Harvey.

"Would *you* fight for your country, Harvey Stone?"

"I'm different."

"How are you different? You're British?"

"Yes. But I..." Harvey paused before he said too much.

"You're what?"

"I'm just different. That's all you need to know."

"I don't need you to tell me you're different, Harvey. I knew it when I first saw you."

"When you were hiding in a ditch?" said Harvey. "Not very military, is it? Unless the French do things differently to the British?"

With a tug of the make-shift bandage, Gabriella pulled the two ends tight, watching as Harvey's face showed no signs of pain or discomfort.

"You're done," said Gabriella. She jabbed at Harvey with the knife before spinning it in her hand and offering him the handle. "You didn't even flinch. I could have killed you right here."

"If you were going to kill me, you would have done it long before you dressed my wound," said Harvey, as he pulled his cargo pants up.

Gabriella gave his body a farewell glance then met Harvey's eyes as they caught her in the act. She handed him a bottle of water, a silent gesture, acknowledging that she meant no harm. Then she sat down beside him and looked out over the town of Saint-Pierre as the first evening lights turned on.

"Is this why you brought me here? For the view?" said Harvey.

"It might be," said Gabriella. "Or I might be trying to seduce you."

The comment caught Harvey's attention enough to raise an eyebrow.

"Why don't you seduce me with Kane's plans?"

"Are you playing hard to get?"

"I'm playing impossible to get."

"The best guys always do," said Gabriella. She tried to stand, but she dizzied and fell back to the ground, steadying herself with her hands on the grass. A fresh wave of nausea washed over her.

"What's wrong?" asked Harvey.

"Nothing," said Gabriella. "It will pass, I am sure."

"Is this the effects of the drug?" said Harvey. "You don't look unstoppable right now."

"I said it will pass," said Gabriella, a little sharply.

Harvey didn't reply.

"Do you see the church tower?" said Gabriella, wiping her eyes and swallowing the acid at the back of her throat.

"West of the marina?" Harvey replied, with one eye on Gabriella.

"Yes," said Gabriella. "Two-man sniper team. From there, they'll see the entire armed procession coming into town. That's the fall-back plan. Do you see the row of buildings on the east side of the marina where the police cars blocked our escape?"

"Low-rise. What are they? Shops?"

"Restaurants," said Gabriella. "The procession will drive straight past them. One two-man team will take out the rear guard vehicles."

"What will that do?" said Harvey. "Why not take out the front vehicles?"

"He wants them to run. There's a protocol when you're guarding the prime minister. The security detail will be small. They will try to get the family out of the town. But if there is only one way out and it is blocked by Kane's Army, they will have no choice but to continue to the marina."

"Two men plus two in the church tower? He'll need more than that. How many men does he have?"

"Less than he did before, thanks to you," said Gabriella. "The final two-man team will ambush them from the fish market. They'll close in as he approaches with the first team bringing up the rear. The prime minister will have nowhere to go."

"Who's ordering the hit?" asked Harvey.

"No-one knows but Kane and the man with the cheque book," said Gabriella. "My guess would be the resistance."

"The resistance?" Harvey felt a smile creep across his tired face.

"The resistance is still strong, Monsieur Stone. They are angry. Too long have they waited in the shadows."

"And what do you get out of this?" said Harvey. "If you don't want to fight for your country, why are you doing this?"

"That's easy," said Gabriella. "I get Kane off my back, for one. But perhaps more importantly, I get to do something significant. It's not every day you get to save your country, Harvey."

"And if we fail?" asked Harvey.

"If we fail and the prime minister is killed, the country will fall. The revolution will destroy us."

"So there's a patriot inside you somewhere?"

Gabriella considered her response. She lay back and let the cold sweat run its course then rolled onto her side to face him.

"I am not a patriot, Harvey Stone. I am just a girl who longs for peace and a simple life. That is all."

―――――

"I don't know how much longer I can hold on," said Gabriella.

Harvey slowed and pulled the bike into a side street one block away from the fish market. He killed the engine then let his mind adjust to the silence before stepping off, searching high on the rooftops for black uniforms against the night sky. But he could only see the dark clouds of a winter storm.

The sound of a body slumping to the ground behind him caused Harvey to spin.

Gabriella lay with her face on the concrete, unable to move. She gave a little moan as Harvey reached beneath each of her limp arms and pulled her out of sight against a white-washed wall.

He sat her up, loosened the top that he'd given her earlier that day, and felt for a pulse.

It was racing.

He placed his hand against her forehead and felt the burn of fever, damp to the touch but moist with a layer of cool sweat.

"Gabriella," whispered Harvey, checking left and right. "We need to move."

But Gabriella didn't respond.

Her head rolled to one side, and a line of thick saliva crept from her open mouth, forming a string that reached the ground. Seeing an alleyway between two boat yards, Harvey scooped her up in his arms, found a dark corner between two bins and lay her down out of sight.

"Gabriella, wake up," said Harvey, and gave her face a gentle slap.

She moaned and opened her eyes. The dim light caught the moist tears that formed and rolled across her face.

"What's wrong with you?" whispered Harvey, aware that Kane's men would be close by.

"I need something," said Gabriella.

She reached out a shaky hand to cling to Harvey's jacket.

"You don't need anything, Gabriella. Get yourself up. We've got work to do."

"I can't," replied Gabriella, letting her hand slip from Harvey's jacket and fall to the ground. "Go on without me. I just need to rest."

"This is what the drug does?" asked Harvey.

"I'm sorry," replied Gabriella, her body tensing as if every muscle in her body called for the drug. "Go on without me. I'll be here."

"What can I do?"

But Gabriella didn't respond. Her eyes closed and her head fell against the wall. Her shallow breaths and racing pulse were the only indication of life.

"Gabriella, what can I do?"

Again, she offered no response.

Harvey checked the street to the left and right. A few Christmas lights adorned the windows of whitewashed houses. The bare roads waited with open arms for the prime minister's arrival. Only the trees that rocked in the growing wind gave sign that the scene wasn't a picture postcard.

Leaving Gabriella in the shadows, Harvey made his way along the road, keeping to the pockets of darkness. The first drops of the approaching storm dotted his leather jacket, leaving black holes in the dust.

The aroma from the fish market hit Harvey before he saw the building. Two cats stopped in their tracks then fled when Harvey dropped from the chain link fence. He remained crouched, watching for movement or light, but found none. A single black SUV was parked beside the main building, which Harvey gauged to be the size of half a football pitch.

Approaching from the shadows, Harvey stepped up to the car. It was empty. But the front was still warm. Droplets of rain fell onto its glossy paintwork, landing with the sound of tiny tapping fingers.

Then, loud and alien in the night, a metal bar slid across the two sliding doors beside the car. The right hand door to the main building screeched into life. Harvey threw himself against the wall as a curtain of light spilled across the ground, illuminating puddles of rain that had already begun to form on the rough concrete.

A man stepped out and exhaled, taking a breath of fresh air. The smell of old fish met Harvey's nostrils stronger than before. Dressed in the familiar black uniform and black boots, the man turned his face up to the rain to refresh himself. On a strap around his neck, an MP-5 hung behind his back, and a handgun was fixed to his chest.

He pulled a cigarette from a pack then stuffed them into his breast pocket before flicking open a zippo lighter. The flame cast a dancing orange light on the man's rough skin then vanished as he slapped the lighter shut and pocketed it.

Harvey took a single step toward him.

But the man's radio broke the silence.

"Alpha-two, this is Alpha-one. Come back."

A plume of thin, grey smoke vanished into the air as he pulled his radio from a pouch on his belt.

Harvey crept through the shadows behind him.

"Alpha-two receiving," replied the man.

"How are you feeling, Alpha-one?"

"I haven't taken it yet. Have you?"

"No, not yet. I'm not one hundred percent sure about injecting myself if I'm honest."

"Same," replied Alpha-two. "I'll use it when I have to. When is the attack due?"

"I have no idea. But keep your eyes peeled. Charlie-two says the boogeyman is out there tonight."

"The boogeyman or Santa Claus?"

"The boogeyman, Alpha-two. You're on the naughty list. Remember?"

"How could I forget?" said Alpha-two, taking a long pull on his cigarette. "I'm out back. It's all clear. I think the smell will keep him away."

"Get back inside. Control your zone. Charlie-two seems to think this guy is good."

Alpha-two exhaled a cloud of smoke, looked left and right, and then raised the radio to his mouth.

"I guess he's on the naughty list too then?"

"Back inside, Alpha-two. Over."

Alpha-two dropped his cigarette to the ground beside the car. It landed with a hiss before the man crushed it beneath his boot. He turned and stopped in his tracks as Harvey pushed the tip of his blade under the man's chin and up into his mouth.

Wide-eyed, Alpha-two inhaled his last breath as he tried to push Harvey's hands away. But a single kick sideways into the man's knee took him down onto the wet ground. Harvey knelt on his chest, released his knife and eased the man's suffering with a slash across his throat.

"Six hours, Jones," said Kane. "Six hours until the prime minister arrives and we become the most celebrated men in France. Are we ready?"

"The men are in position, sir," said Jones.

The sound of footsteps on the steel mesh mezzanine walkway that ran around the perimeter of the pharmaceutical factory was percussive in the open space. Bright lights hung from the white painted ceiling, illuminating the glass vials and casting monstrous bloody shapes across the smooth, white worktops.

"Six months, Jones. Six months of watching those scientists day after day, failure after failure, excuse after excuse. And we finally have it. Nothing can stop us now."

"What about the girl?" asked Jones.

"She'll come crawling back. She's been dosed with SFS for the past month. Her body needs it. She can't live without it."

"And Stone?" said Jones. "The man has taken out three teams already. He'll come for us here and we don't have the men to stop him."

Kane pushed off the handrail where he'd been leaning, looked across at his number two, and smiled the smile of success.

"Follow me, Jones," said Kane, as he descended the steel staircase. "There's something I want you to see."

On the wall beside a pair of double doors was a large exit button. Jones hit it and the electric doors opened. A loud electronic alarm sounded to alert anybody in the factory that someone was entering.

The doors opened into a small cleaning chamber; as soon as the electric doors closed behind Kane and Jones, it clicked into action. A loud hiss from above indicated that air was being sucked out of the room. Tiny jets on the walls issued clouds of chemically enhanced steam that sanitised a person's clothes on entry and exit. A blast of fresh oxygen cleared the air and another set of doors opened along with the sound of another loud electronic alarm.

With his hands behind his back, Kane enjoyed the tap of

his heels against the painted concrete floor in the long corridor. He savoured the lines of glass-walled observation rooms, control rooms and cells, where the test subjects had been kept like dogs.

Like a king overlooking his kingdom, Kane admired his creation. But as he stepped up to observation room three and stared down at the ruination that Doctor Farrow had become, Kane felt his power grow a little more. Just like Frankenstein pulling the switch and seeing his collation of dead body parts twitch for the first time, Kane recognised the monster he had created.

"Is that Farrow?" asked Jones, peering through the glass with a look of both disgust and intrigue.

"It *was* Doctor Farrow, Jones," replied Kane, admiring his work. "I don't know what you'd call it now."

"How many doses has he had?"

"Five," replied Kane. "Five doses of SFS in under five hours. It's the most anybody has ever survived, even if it is the prototype."

"You call that surviving?" said Jones. "Is he even human anymore?"

As if on cue, a hand slapped against the reinforced window. Its outline was traced by a cloud of breath that fogged the glass.

"I don't know what you'd call it now," said Kane, feeling the corners of his mouth rise with success. "But God help anyone who stands in its way."

11

COMMUNICATION BREAKDOWN

A CRACK OF THUNDER DRAGGED GABRIELLA FROM HER slumber in a panic. Her body shook with the cold, aching for something she knew would kill her. But still, one more hit was all she would need.

Another rumble in the black sky above and the sound of rain like white noise hissed at her from every direction. A single flash of lightning lit the night. Its bright fork reached down and struck the earth somewhere far away behind the unmistakable silhouette of the fish market.

It was a sign.

The fish market was large and plain. It was the only building with lights on along the street save for the flashing colours of Christmas decorations that brought cheer to a world far removed from Gabriella's mind.

She rolled to her side and pushed herself up to one knee. Then, using the wall for support, she stood. A rush of blood rocked her and a surge of nausea rose from her stomach; burning acid seeped into her mouth until she bent, vomited, and spat the acrid remnants to the wet ground.

Her feet moved of their own accord. Her hands crept

along the wall to her side, keeping her from falling. Her vision blurred at the edges; just a plain white, square building focused in its centre.

Somewhere inside that place was everything she needed.

The chain link fence rattled when she fell against it then supported her as she pulled herself along and sought a way through. A gate, a hole or a break.

But she found no such entry.

Another flash of lightning struck simultaneously to the thunder that cracked, angry and deep, above Gabriella. Her body began to climb up the fence while her mind still wondered at the sky. She rolled over the top and fell to the ground in a daze, unhurt. Then, like the first land creatures, she crawled across the wet ground, weak and with an unrelenting hunger.

She clambered onto a motionless body in black. Her fingers pried open his pockets. Her hands felt the seams of his clothes, bloodied from the slash across his neck. But she found nothing and fell back to the ground. Something stabbed at her arm.

A shard of glass.

Fingering the wound, she plucked the tiny glass fragment from her skin, feeling its smooth surface. Then she recognised its tight curve.

With a gasp, she dropped the glass and began searching the wet ground, but found only the remains of a broken vial, which had been crushed by a boot. Its contents had spilled onto the rain-soaked ground and been washed away to a nearby drain.

The ache in her heart weighed heavy as she closed her tear-filled eyes and lay down staring up at the sky.

Bright fluorescent light flickered through the open factory door, lighting Gabriella's face in flashes of anguish mirrored by the distant lightning. She rolled to her side and stared through the gap. The view offered her little more than rows upon rows of white, shiny benches stood on a shiny, white, tiled floor. A shadow rose against the furthest wall then shrank again as if a rat had ventured into the open, scurrying toward a lamp, then retreated back to the safety of the cold, dark corners.

Gabriella crawled closer, rising to her feet, then peered inside.

At one end of the building were huge shutter doors, where the fresh fish would be unloaded from the boats. Giant hooks hung from thick chains on beams that would lift the cargo to be sorted, cleaned and then sold.

A single drop of water fell from someplace high, perhaps a leak in the roof. It landed on a bench, where a seller would display his fish, facing out towards the customer with his mouth open and blank wide eyes staring at a palm full of Euros.

Blank, wide eyes.

Gabriella knew the empty stare.

She'd seen it in the girls with whom she'd shared the past month of her life. They'd been pumped full of chemicals and forced to run until the only way for their bodies to survive was to shut down the very organs that kept them alive.

The blank stare.

The blank stare of her father while batons continued to beat him even after all life had slipped away. Strong hands had pulled Gabriella off him, where she lay protecting his body. But not for her own safety. Instead, crazed uniformed men had rained down blows on her instead.

The crack of bones echoed in the empty space. A rattle of chains responded. Gabriella spun. Her feet scraped against the screed floor, answering the crack with the squeak of rubber.

Blinking the blur from her eyes until a fragment of focus

formed, she made her way toward the shutters, the shadows and the crack of bones. Accompanied only by the rasp of her breath and the sound of her hand brushing along the benches, the noises guided her in her semi-blind state.

A dark, glossy shadow formed between the two shutter doors, a spreading blemish seeping out on the white tiled floor. Its black fingers found the joins between the tiles and ran between them, spreading the word of darkness.

A finger of the spreading shadow touched Gabriella's running shoe. Then it split to run around each side of her foot. She stepped away, horrified at the sticky blood. But something touched her shoulder. Startled, she spun, and came face to face with a tongueless man. He stared back at her in the flickering light with soulless eyes wide with fear.

Moving away from the atrocity, Gabriella fought to calm her breathing. She slipped in the puddle of blood and fell to the floor. But she continued to scramble away backwards on her hands, searching around her for the culprit in the shadows.

But curiosity drew her attention to the dead man. She stared in awe at his lifeless form. A hook had been buried into the back of the man's skull; the chain above from which it hung was taut.

She crawled closer.

The body swung back at her touch then rocked forward.

Blank with wide eyes.

The flickering light cast flashes of monstrous shadows as Gabriella fumbled her way around the rows of benches. The girl who had demonstrated rare strength and courage now appeared feeble in Harvey's eyes. He was driven on by something far more powerful than her drug, which had only proven to grip her and render her unconscious.

She jumped at the touch of the body and slipped in its blood.

Harvey remained curious and hidden in the shadows.

Scrambling to her feet, her bloodied hands searched the corpse, ripping open pockets and dropping items onto the sticky floor until she found what she was looking for. She stopped and gasped.

As if she'd discovered some long, lost treasure, Gabriella pulled her hand from the pocket with a tenderness contrasting the frantic searching she had performed moments before. Cupping the item in both hands, she held it up to the light as if her disbelief required a visual inspection and confirmation.

Between her finger and thumb, Gabriella held a vial containing a dark, red liquid.

Seconds later, she began another search of the man's pocket. She found a small pouch and set to work. She ripped open the flap. The rasp of Velcro was sudden and violent, and lost to the incessant pitter-patter of rain outside, on the roof, and against the steel shutter doors.

A practiced hand prepared the syringe with surprising speed, but her haste and shaky fingers dropped the vial onto the bench. It rolled away from her.

"No," she whispered.

Seeing the vial pick up speed, Gabriella headed for the end of the bench. She dropped the syringe, pushed past the swinging body, and reached for the vial. Missing her aim, she slipped in the bloody puddle. She clung to the surface as her feet danced then found grip on a dry tile.

But it was too late.

The vial teetered on the edge of the bench, teasing

Gabriella as she stood frozen, not daring to move in case she tipped the balance and sent the vial crashing to the floor.

"Stay," said Gabriella.

Her voice was a low whisper. She spoke as if the vial would hear her command. Reaching across the bench and sliding across the smooth surface, her hand then raised like the head of a cobra, poised, ready to strike and trap the vial.

The fluorescent light above her buzzed with electricity. The vial toyed tentatively with Gabriella's state of mind, daring her to make her move.

She struck.

The light blinked off and on.

And the vial fell into Harvey's hand.

Gabriella slid to the floor as if the hunt had taken every last morsel of energy, leaving her without hope. The tears began first, silent as if Gabriella mourned the loss of a friend. Her weak grip on the bench released and her knees buckled as if the weight of the loss was too much for them to bear.

She sank to the floor.

Harvey stepped from the shadows.

"Get up, Gabriella," said Harvey.

His voice startled her. She fell back onto her hands and scrambled away from him through the blood.

A crack of thunder outside tore through the night. She pushed back against the bench and pulled her knees up to her chin.

The light flickered off.

Harvey moved closer, watching her head twitch left and right. Her eyes blinked for focus then stared at the darkness and blurred shadows.

"Who's there?" said Gabriella.

Harvey didn't reply.

"I said, who's there?" said Gabriella, louder than before, as if her aggression would elicit a response.

She pushed herself to one knee, held onto the bench and stood, peering around for movement.

"How bad do you need it?" said Harvey.

He moved through the darkness as she placed the voice and stared into the shadows.

"How bad do you need a fix?" he asked.

But Gabriella couldn't reply.

"Are you dying?" asked Harvey.

"I don't know," said Gabriella, her voice low and weak, and her eyes glistening in the half-light. "This is the longest I have been without it. My body is shutting down. I can feel it happening inside me. It's like small pieces of me are turning off."

"You're weak," said Harvey.

"He did this to me," said Gabriella. "He made me this way."

"Why don't you come and get it?" said Harvey, stepping into view holding the vial out for Gabriella's poisoned mind to find.

"Give it to me, Harvey."

"You can have it," said Harvey, as Gabriella's hands reached forward onto the floor.

Her legs straightened behind her, raising her body as a leopard might prepare to attack. Gabriella inched forward, hand over hand, footstep by footstep, until she stared up at Harvey like a wild animal, only a pounce away.

"You want it?" asked Harvey.

He opened his hand and held it out an arm's length away from Gabriella. Her eyes followed the vial, her body tensed, and her breathing slowed.

She struck, snatching at Harvey's palm. But he closed his fist around the vial, reached down with his free hand, and took hold of Gabriella's neck, gripping tight and lifting her into the air before slamming her into the shutters.

Gabriella's nails scratched at Harvey's face. Her feet kicked out at him until he slammed her once more into the shutters to silence her. Gabriella's top lip retracted, exposing her teeth in a snarl. A visceral growl emerged from her throat.

She spat in Harvey's face.

"Give it to me," said Gabriella, panting and struggling to breathe through Harvey's grip.

Harvey leaned in close, searching her dilated eyes to see if the blackness held any sign of colour.

"You're going to take me to Kane," said Harvey. "You do that for me, and you can have as much as you need."

———

"Bravo-one, come back," said Jones, as he paced the court-yard, searching for the best radio signal. "Bravo-one, come back. This is Charlie-two."

Kane leaned against the door under the porch canopy with a cigarette in his hand, eying his second in command as he fought to maintain an expression of control and composure. Yet Jones stomped around in the rain, his anger and frustration getting the better of him.

"Alpha-one, come back," said Jones. "I repeat, Alpha-one, this is Charlie-two. Come back."

A surge of static crackled through the radio's circuitry then faded.

"Problems, Jones?" asked Kane, as he exhaled a cloud of smoke and watched the atmosphere dilute it until nothing was left but the tainted scent.

"Nothing I can't handle, sir," replied Jones, raising the radio to his mouth once more. "Tango-one, come back. Tango-one, this is Charlie-two. Talk to me."

"He's out there," said Kane, before a crackled voice came over the airwaves.

"Charlie-two, this is Tango-one. Copy."

"Sit-rep?" said Jones.

"Nothing to report. I have a clear view of the marina, the yacht, and most of the town. It's all quiet on the western front."

"Tango-one, have you got eyes on the fish market?"

"Charlie-two, copy. That's a positive. I have eyes on the fish market. Not a creature is stirring, not even a mouse."

"Drop the Christmas jokes, Tango-one. Do you have eyes on Alpha team?" said Jones, then glanced back at Kane.

"Charlie-two, this is Tango-one. No visual on Alpha-one or Alpha-two. Nothing to report, Sarge."

Jones stared up at the sky, squinting as the rain drops bounced from his face.

"You're worried, Jones," said Kane, as he flicked his cigarette butt across the courtyard, watching the little orange ember spin then disappear in a hiss when it landed in a puddle. "I've seen that look before."

"I'm sending in Bravo team," said Jones. "Alpha team are the strike force. The fish market is the perfect place for an ambush. I need comms with them."

"You're also leaving the door open," said Kane. "If Stone is in there, he'll escape. Isn't it better to contain him?"

"All units stand by," said Jones into the radio.

Jones glanced up at Kane then lowered his eyes to the ground.

"We've got a few hours before the prime minister rolls into town, sir. I'm nine men down, and I've lost contact with my strike team. Stone or no Stone, I need my strike team in place and I need comms."

"Do you think Alpha team can take him down?" asked Kane.

Jones nodded. But it was not the nod of a confident

solider sending his men into battle. Instead, it was the nod of a man hedging his bets and playing the odds.

Pulling his packet of cigarettes from his pocket, Kane removed the last one then crushed the empty pack and tossed it to the ground.

"How well do you remember that night?" asked Kane.

Jones looked back at him. His face was only half-lit by the spotlights on the roof of the building and rain dripped from his nose.

"Afghanistan?"

"Is there another night you have in mind?"

Jones shook his head. "I relive that night at least three times a week, sir."

"Three times a week?" said Kane, in surprise. "I think about it every day."

"Have you thought about seeing a counsellor?" asked Jones. He didn't smile at his own joke, even though both men knew the idea was out of the question.

"I remember when we got the call over the radio," said Kane. "I remember your face, and that was the first time I ever saw you falter."

"With all due respect, sir, I'd have to contradict that statement."

"Permission denied, Jones," said Kane, and stepped into the rain. "Your decision that night cost men their lives. Your failure to make the call at the right time killed my men, the army's men. Your decision earned us all a discharge."

Kane put his hands behind his back, held his chest out, and walked behind Jones. His second in command remained resolute, facing the doorway. He was always the model soldier.

"Stand up straight, man," said Kane.

Jones stood to attention. "Every decision we made in that hell-hole cost men their lives, sir," he said. "That was our night to lose lives. It was an ambush. You know as well as I do that we'd have lost every single man if I hadn't made a decision at all."

"Quite right," said Kane. "Quite right indeed. That's why I stood by you. That's why, regardless of the friends and comrades we all lost, the men out there tonight stood by you, because you made a decision."

"Innocent people died, sir. That's a fact I'll live with for the rest of my life. But fifteen good soldiers came home."

"They slaughtered a village, Jones."

"They were hiding militants," he replied. "They may not have had AK-forty-sevens in their hands, but they were hiding the men who did."

"That's not how the Queen's army works though, is it, Jones? That's not standard operating procedure."

"Standard procedure would have killed every single man on our squad. My decision saved a handful of them and we completed the mission."

"And that handful of men are out there right now, Jones. They're facing a lunatic who is pulling your team apart. What are you going to do about it?"

"We're going to take him down, sir."

"But what about the prime minister?" said Kane. "What about the mission?"

Jones hesitated.

"Tick-tock, Jones. The prime minister is on his way here now and there's a madman picking your men off. What's more important? Your men or the mission?"

"My men, sir."

Surprised by the response, Kane stopped his pacing, but allowed Jones to continue.

"Without my men, there is no mission," said Jones. "Without my men, all this would be for nothing."

"So what are you going to do about it?"

Jones didn't reply.

"It's time for SFS," said Kane.

"They don't need it, sir. Not yet. I can't risk them hitting withdrawal before the prime minister arrives."

"That's your call, Jones. But remember, if you make the wrong decision again, I might not be so..." Kane hovered, searching for the right word. "Forgiving. Do you think Alpha team can take him down without SFS?"

"I have every confidence in them, sir."

"Then do it," said Kane. "It's decision time."

Jones turned on the heels of his boots to face Kane. He held his stare in an effort to convey a renewed confidence in his decision. Then he raised the radio.

"Alpha-one, this is Charlie-two. Come back."

Silence was broken only by the flow of static.

"Alpha-one, this is Charlie-two. Come back."

"Charlie-two?" came the reply.

"Alpha-one, respond using radio protocol."

"I don't really know about protocol," said the voice. "But you're running out of men, Charlie-two."

12

COMFORTABLY NUMB

The wide, leather seat of the black SUV sucked Gabriella from a world of pain, cramps, cold sweats and nausea as her muscles begged for a sharp stab into her skin and the release of SFS. She slipped into a world of soft, blurred dream-like visions as if she was standing giddily on a precipice. One step forward would snatch her from everything she knew, a world where trees grew tall and carpets of green lined the earth beneath the summer sun. One step back would dismiss the unknown that beckoned her forward, coaxing her with flashes of potential happiness and the faces of those she had sworn to avenge.

Revenge seemed so far away.

With barely the energy to raise her arm and guide Harvey Stone, she mumbled directions whenever she swayed back to reality. Then she sunk into the warm arms of the soft seat once more to search the darkness for another glimpse of her father and brother.

Just one more glimpse of their faces. One more word from their mouths. The sound of their voices.

The dashboard lights faded and the outline of Harvey's

taut face melded into the darkness that enveloped her vision once more. Gabriella embraced the tightness in her chest and the grip on her stomach as memories span around her like an old film reel, spliced with desire and longing.

She saw her father working his garden in his favourite tan corduroys, braces and a white under-vest. His paunch was on display like a trophy. He was unashamed, a man who had raised two children, faced the trials of life, and emerged on the other side with just a bloated tummy for a wound. Gabriella stepped from the house, lifted a hanging grape vine from the archway that divided the garden, and stepped through into her father's vegetable patch. It was his pride and joy. Rows of shallots and carrots, romaine lettuce and leeks, cauliflower and zucchini were bordered by trellised walls of berries and grapes. Butterflies danced from flower to flower and the song of the birds hung on the breeze that tickled the tops of the fat apple trees beyond the garden.

He leaned on his garden fork, fanning himself with his cap, and smiled at Gabriella as the summer sun shone across his tanned skin. He opened his arms as she approached, welcoming her in for one of those long, tight hugs, his hands stained with the rich soil and his warm eyes following her every step of the way.

But the smile faded.

His face twitched.

The mud on his hands turned red when he raised them to his face. A baton came down, striking his flesh and breaking his bones. The garden was gone, replaced by a busy Parisian street. The tall walls of grapes and berries morphed into lines of men in helmets with riot shields and batons. The bright flowers in Gabriella's memory that her father had so lovingly planted and nurtured became the bright vests of the angry, the upset, the beaten and the trampled. The wandering smoke of the smouldering compost blended into clouds of tear gas.

Her father's face faded away, hidden with each strike of the batons and every kick of the heavy, black boots that stamped on Gabriella's memories. She'd tried to pull the men off him but they were too strong for her. She'd tried to cling to her father's bloodied clothes, but his corduroy pants slipped through her hands and he disappeared into the cloud of tear gas, leaving only a bed of memories.

Inside Gabriella, a seed of hate had taken root. Its gnarled and twisted fingers had violated the deepest parts of her mind, leaving nothing but the bitter taste of revenge.

The memories faded away as consciousness emerged from the darkness. But no matter how hard Gabriella fought it, the lights on the dashboard became clearer. The outline of Harvey Stone's face became defined. The incessant rain on the windows and car roof hissed like white noise.

"You're back," said Harvey. He glanced across at her before returning his attention to the wet road. "I'm going to need some directions soon."

But slumber still held Gabriella with a single, bony finger. Unfinished thoughts and memories amalgamated into a bizarre reality. That man wasn't Harvey; that was Francis, her brother. It was Christmas time, long ago, when they were driving through the night for Gabriella to see the Paris lights.

"Remember, Gabriella, you must not tell mother or father about this," Francis had said. "It is our little secret."

Curled in the passenger seat of her brother's car, Gabriella had dozed. The rolling fields and endless railways made it seem as if they hadn't travelled a single mile, despite a full night of driving.

"I won't tell them," said Gabriella. "Will we see the Eiffel Tower?"

"We will, and you will marvel in its beauty, Gabriella."

"And the Notre Dame? Will we see the Notre Dame?"

"Never again will you find such beauty in something so grotesque, little sister."

"And will there be Christmas lights at the Champs-Elysees?"

"Brighter than the stars in the sky, Gabriella," said Francis. "Go to sleep. We will be there in a few hours. I will wake you."

Sleep had welcomed her into its warm, outstretched arms with the promise of everything she loved. A blanket had covered her and tucked beneath her arm was Antoine, a fluffy, blue rabbit with one eye and a broad smile, always a smile.

A strong hand had gripped her and wrenched her from sleep, pinning her down so she couldn't move. Blinding lights turned the woken world white. The thump of rotor blades just meters from the roof of the car pounded her ears like the beating of her heart, heavy in her chest.

"Hold on, Gabriella. Don't be scared," said Francis. "This is going to be a little rough."

She woke with a start, sucking in air. For the first time, she saw the dashboard clearly and vividly. A hand pinned her to the seat. Harvey's face was so defined even in the meagre light beyond the window.

"Hold on, Gabriella," said Harvey. "This is going to be a little rough."

Two guards in black uniforms stepped into the road and opened fire as soon as Harvey slid the SUV into the driveway of the old factory. Bullets shattered the windscreen and punctured the engine block. A violent hiss of angry steam burst from the front of the car, obscuring Harvey's view. But he planted his right foot and aimed at the two men, who continued to fire, unafraid of the two tons of car that accelerated towards them. Crouching with his head low and peering above the dashboard, Harvey felt the car slam into the two bodies. One of them was forced beneath the wheels, lifting the car to one side with a sickening bounce. The second guard rolled onto the bonnet. His face was a bloodied mess as he clung to the wipers and raised his head to stare through the shattered glass at Harvey.

Holding on with one hand, the man began to punch through the broken windscreen, ripping his skin with each blow. Undeterred, he continued to force a hole, making it larger and larger. Harvey accelerated harder, weaving from side to side to shake the man from the car. But he held on with ruined hands and rare tenacity.

At the end of the driveway, a small complex of buildings issued the only light in an otherwise black landscape. The buildings on the left and right formed the sides of a U with a central building behind connecting them to form a central courtyard. Aiming the car at the end of the left building, Harvey dropped down into third gear. He gave everything the car had as the guard continued to hammer his way through the glass.

Seeing Harvey's intentions, the man doubled his efforts, sliding his body around and bringing his heavy boots into play. The heel of a black boot burst through the glass and kicked at Harvey's face. It retracted for another kick and the guard maneuvered for better purchase.

But it was too late for him.

The front wheels hit the curb stone and lifted the car into the air. The rear wheels followed, sending the vehicle soaring inches from the grass border and smashing into the end of the building. It powered into the laboratory from the outside.

Rows of benches blocked the car's path, but it bounced on the laboratory floor, continuing the momentum and ploughing through anything that stood in its way. The benches, dozens of glass vials and various pieces of lab equipment scattered across the floor.

A set of double doors stood at the far end of the lab. The car hissed and moaned with the effort, but Harvey forced it forward, smashing into the doors and wedging into the gap.

The engine died with a blast of angry steam.

A hiss of gas blasted from the walls.

The guard fell from the front of the car.

"What have you done?" said Gabriella, trying to force the car door open, but finding herself trapped. "You're insane."

But there was no time for discussion.

Two men dressed in black stepped into the corridor in front. They ducked through separate side doors then peered around the corners, releasing a three-round burst of gunfire each, which dotted the front of the car.

"We need to go," said Harvey. He raised his leg to kick the remains of the windscreen out from its frame. "Now, Gabriella. Move."

But she didn't follow.

Harvey rolled from the front of the car and clambered into the doorway of a sample room just as more bullets peppered the car. He pulled his knife from his belt; it was his only remaining weapon. With his back against the wall, he waited with his eyes closed, calming his breathing and listening for the approaching guards.

The heavy boots on the linoleum floor came in waves of five. First one set then the other. Harvey pictured the two men running five steps, stopping, and then dropping to a crouch to provide cover for the next man to progress forward.

A flash of movement came from inside the car. Then nothing. Harvey strived to see through the steam that billowed from the grill, but saw nothing. He peered into the corridor.

The first guard stepped into view, his attention focused on the car, searching through the billowing steam for signs of life. A jab of Harvey's knife to the man's throat sent a spurt of blood across the floor. His partner opened fired. Harvey pulled the dying man in front of him and rushed the second guard using the twitching body as a shield.

The guard hesitated. Instinct prevented him from shooting his partner. The force of Harvey and the body colliding with the guard sent him reeling backwards and through a glass wall into a small office. As the shattered safety glass rained down upon the two men and the body, Harvey began an onslaught of violent punches into the guard's face and throat.

But each blow seemed only to anger the guard. His strength seemed to increase the angrier he became until he forced Harvey up with two powerful hands on his throat. Dragging Harvey to his feet, he slammed him into the wall. Harvey continued to punch, finding the sweet spot every time. But each well-placed blow angered the guard more and more until, tired of the charade, he threw Harvey across the room like a rag doll. Harvey crashed onto a wooden desk, breaking it in half, and landed in a pile of splinters on the floor.

But there was no reprise.

The man was unstoppable.

He stepped into view, kicking away the remains of the desk, and grabbed Harvey once more by the throat with a grip like iron. Bright lights sparkled in Harvey's vision. A darkness formed at the edge of his sight. As the guard dragged Harvey from the office, Harvey's boots struggled for purchase on linoleum floor. He knew that the man's steely grip was squeezing the life from him.

Then a burst of glass and the roar of something wild and new filled the space.

The man's grip released Harvey, dropping him to the floor where he rolled onto his front, clutching his throat. He stared up at the source of the distraction.

But even Harvey was unprepared for what he saw.

A man with his forehead caved in, the skin of his face shredded, and his naked torso, stripped of clothing, pulsing as if his body played host to something far wilder than mankind, rose to stand. He emitted a scream so unnatural and inhuman that Harvey squeezed his eyes closed at the intrusion and lay perfectly still.

The guard began to backtrack as the disfigured man took a single, unstable step. He appeared to sniff at the air, then grunted in delight at the fear his sense found. The ruined man took another step, then another, finding his flow and balance. As momentum built, he began to run. He passed Harvey in a flash of anger, his bare feet leaving a trail of blood.

The SUV lodged into the wall blocked the guard's exit. Scrambling, the terrified man found his partner's rifle lying dormant on the floor. He turned and fired.

But it was too late.

The ruined beast of a man collided with the guard, pinning him to the front of the car. He reached for his prize, gripped the man's head in both hands, and smashed his skull into the bonnet until it broke with a sickening crack.

Stunned by the events, Harvey began to move away. He rose to his feet with no sudden movements and stepped back-ward, creeping further into the building. But, as if enhanced senses alerted the ruined man, his head snapped around to face the corridor. His tongue, half-chewed, licked his lips. And his eyes, wild and red with blood, met Harvey's.

Harvey returned the stare.

The blood-soaked creature took a step towards Harvey.

Staring through a pair of double doors, Kane grinned as Doctor Farrow dropped the remains of Zulu-one and set his deranged sights on Harvey Stone, who was backing away along the corridor.

"Now we'll see the real power of SFS," said Kane. "Even if it is just the prototype."

The doors rattled as Stone tried to pull them open. But Jones slid his MP-5 through the handles, blocking his escape. Stone's angered face appeared at the small window then vanished behind a fog of breath. As the condensation faded, something hard and heavy slammed into the doors, and loud, feverish grunts accompanied the dull thuds of viscous beating.

"How long do you think he'll last?" asked Jones, standing beside Kane and watching with the same enthused awe as Harvey Stone and the drug-fuelled remains of Doctor Farrow rolled away from the doors along the corridor, locked in battle.

"I'm surprised he's lasted this long," replied Kane.

Harvey rolled on top and forced his thumb into Farrow's eye socket. But the move only antagonised the doctor. A surge of power threw Stone to one side, where he rolled to his feet in time for Farrow to launch another attack. The pair slammed against the glass wall of an observation room. From Kane's viewpoint behind the safety doors, he saw the glass panel flex with their weight. The two men, locked in a wrestle, pulled each other to the floor, grappling for control.

Farrow found himself on top.

The punches came hard and fast with no clarity as to which was Farrow's leading arm and which was his trailing follow-up punch. Each blow rocked Stone's head from side to side, and with each hit, he weakened a little more.

But there was more to the man who, over the last two days, had taken down Kane's Army one by one. There was a resilience uncommon in any man Kane had ever seen before. He had a tenacity so pure and raw, Kane couldn't help but admire him as he watched the battle play out.

"He won't get up," said Jones. "Nobody can withstand that."

But from their viewpoint, they saw calmness come over Stone. He no longer appeared to fight back. Instead, he absorbed the blows, either waiting for death to take him or his opponent to tire.

"That's it," said Jones.

Stone lay motionless on the bloodied floor, and Farrow rose, searching for a new victim. His eyes fell on Kane and Jones staring at him through the two small windows in the doors.

"Stone is done," said Kane.

"We have a much bigger problem," said Jones.

Farrow's eyes remained fixed on Kane's. His ruined body pulsed as the muscles beneath his flesh tensed and relaxed with the high volume of SFS. A flap of skin hung from Farrow's face. Tiny shards of glass were embedded into the wound and his fractured skull revealed a sickening sight.

"Farrow's tiring," said Jones, re-securing his MP-5 in the door handles. "The SFS must be wearing off. We need to get to the bunker."

"No," replied Kane, his eyes wide with both disappointment and admiration. "Look at him, Jones."

But Jones was backing away from the doors, pulling his handgun from the holster fixed to his chest. "Move away, sir," he said. "If Farrow comes through, I'll take him down."

The tiny round window in the door darkened with

Farrow's shadow. His face appeared at the glass. Torn skin revealed his rear teeth through what was once his cheek. His caved forehead seeped dark, red blood in thick gloops that hung from his brow. And his eyes, redder than any eyes Kane had ever seen, stared deep into his own.

Farrow's hand appeared in the second window pane. The doctor's once soft, gentle skin was now stained with blood. His once slender, precise fingers, the instruments of his profession, were curled, gnarled and tense, and ready to crush anything they gripped.

"Sir, move back," called Jones. "I can take him from here."

But Kane was in awe. He approached the window, stopping inches from Farrow's face, holding his gaze with wonder and fascination. Kane raised his hand, laying it flat against the glass and meeting Farrow's tensed, splayed fingers one for one.

"Sir, don't do it," said Jones. "He's wild. Move back. Let me take him out."

"No," said Kane, snatching his head to face Jones, whose face dropped at the sudden anger. "Lower your weapon, Jones."

But Jones remained with his weapon aimed at the glass.

"I said lower your weapon, Jones," said Kane. "That's an order."

He turned to face Farrow once more, who offered Jones a spiteful glare then returned to meet Kane's eyes, and softened. His head cocked to one side, and his face grimaced as he forced his tense hand flat against the glass, connecting it with Kane's.

With his free hand, Kane reached into his pocket, retrieved the small vial of prototype SFS, and held it up for Farrow to see. The effect was immediate. Farrow's unblinking eyes widened further. A snort fogged the glass and he began scratching at the door, pushing the wood until it bowed.

"Open the door, Jones," said Kane.

"Absolutely not, sir," replied Jones. "You've lost your mind."

"I said open the damn door," replied Kane, and pulled his weapon on Jones. "Now."

Jones glanced at the wall switch that released the electro-magnetic doors, then at Farrow, whose ruined face pressed against the glass watching Jones' every move, and then back to Kane, who held his weapon high with a finger poised over the trigger.

A battle seemed to take place inside Jones' mind as he fought between what he knew was right and everything he'd been taught about respect, trust and loyalty. He took a breath and raised his arm to hit the switch. But at the last minute, he turned his weapon on Kane.

"Sir, I respectfully decline," said Jones, holding his head high.

"You'll open that door if it's the last thing you do," said Kane.

Farrow banged against the glass window.

"Sir, I cannot."

Kane shifted his aim from Jones' chest to his head.

Farrow banged against the door.

"Last chance, Jones."

The doors cracked as Farrow slammed against them; the wood bowed and flexed with his weight.

"Sir, you've lost your mind."

Both men opposed each other, fingers teasing the triggers, in a silent battle of courage until, at last, Jones lowered his weapon.

"For a moment there, I thought you'd forgotten who you were talking to," said Kane. "Drop it."

Jones tossed the handgun to the floor.

"Now open the damn door," said Kane.

Jones stepped forward to the doors, staring at Farrow eye to eye through the glass. He slid the MP-5 from between the handles, pulled the cocking lever, and flicked the safety off.

Bloodshot eyes tracked Jones to the emergency release button on the wall.

The doors flexed as Farrow pressed against the wood.

"Go on, Jones," said Kane.

With the MP-5 raised against Jones' shoulder, he nudged the door release with his elbow.

The doors crashed open and slammed into the walls. Jones stepped back, finger fixed to the trigger, and Doctor Farrow stepped through, sniffing at the air. Soft grunts came from his throat with each rapid breath. His eyes twitched and the muscles on his lean body tensed then relaxed as if on a perpetual cycle. He eyed Jones and took a step forward.

"That's it, Farrow," said Jones, taking a step back. "One more step and I'll put you down like a dog."

But instead of rushing Jones as Kane thought he would, Farrow turned his head sideways, studying the greying man who stood before him.

Farrow let out a cry, opening his mouth as far as his ruined jaw would allow.

Standing his ground, Kane reached into his pocket and removed the little vial of red liquid once more.

Farrow silenced.

"You want this?" asked Kane. Farrow snatched at the vial. But Kane saw the move coming and snapped his hand away. "Now, now, Doctor Farrow, remember your manners."

Farrow retracted his hand like a child, but followed the vial with his eyes like a dog with the promise of a bone.

"Farrow," said Kane, pointing to his own face. "Eyes up here."

Farrow tore his eyes from the vial.

"You want this?" said Kane.

Farrow grunted in confirmation, his jaw muscles so tense, they allowed for no articulation of pronounced words.

Kane glanced across at Jones who was frozen in horror, and then back at Farrow.

"Kill," said Kane.

13

DAZED AND CONFUSED

FROZEN WITH FEAR AND FACING DEATH, GABRIELLA LAY curled on the passenger seat with her feet against the dashboard as a deranged guard clung to the bonnet and tried to force his way through the windscreen. Harvey aimed the car at the building. Her eyes wandered to Harvey, and somehow in all the chaos she admired his control and tenacity. She reached out a hand and rested it on his shoulder, pushing the sickness to one side as the anticipation of feeding her hunger grew.

But the chance of satiating her thirst and her focus faded when the engine suddenly roared and Harvey pushed himself back into the seat. Then came a sense of weightlessness, a peace where time slowed and nothing mattered, until the front of the car smashed through the wall and chaos ensued.

Even as bricks and glass showered down onto the car, Harvey forced an entry through the row of lab benches, pushing further into the building despite the grinding, smoke and strong smell of fuel.

"We need to go," said Harvey. He raised his leg to kick the

remains of the windscreen out from its frame. "Now, Gabriella. Move."

She feigned sickness, exaggerating her incapacitation by curling into a ball and closing her eyes.

"Stay here," said Harvey, and climbed through the space where the windscreen had been.

Harvey hadn't even hit the floor before gunshots sang out in the corridor ahead. Gabriella pushed the chair back and climbed into the rear of the car. She lay out of sight, peering through the rear window at the carnage in the laboratory.

Furniture had been toppled and dozens of vials had smashed onto the floor, forming a puddle in the middle of the room.

Her stomach twisted at the sight as if some monstrous hand squeezed her insides.

She scanned the wreckage for something. Anything. And gasped when her eyes found what she'd been looking for.

Glass shattered in the corridor in front of the car and the grunts and groans of men fighting, furniture being destroyed, and tempers flaring masked the heavy click of Gabriella opening the rear door.

But the sickness still lingered. Despite the thoughts of replenishing her body with another dose, and the joy as she pondered the feeling of it running through her veins, her legs failed to carry her weight.

Inch by inch, Gabriella crawled across broken glass, her body aching and sleep tugging at her consciousness, pulling her mind from the tray of syringes ahead and the single unbroken vial. She reached out, stretching as far as her weakened body would allow, feeling the taut muscles in her stomach pull. The weight of her arm was too heavy to hold. Her fingers fumbled for the tray but pushed it further away. One more shuffle across the floor and she reached it, tipping the tray over to spill its contents onto the floor.

Gabriella lay on her side. Her weak and shaking hands caused the plastic hygiene wrapper to slip through her fingers. She tore at it with her teeth then spat the plastic away.

A scream, wild and savage, echoed from the corridor as she pulled the protective tip from the needle and plunged it into the vial. Nothing else existed as she watched the red liquid fill the syringe chamber.

Something huge crashed into the front of the car. Gabriella's heart jumped into gear as more agonised screams illustrated the scene in the corridor.

A vein, thick and blue, stuck out from her arm as if her body craved the offering, presenting itself to the needle. Her hands, weak and uncontrollable, fumbled with the syringe, and her eyes, laden with the weight of revenge, used every ounce of her energy to remain open.

The needle pierced the skin. The hot feeling as it found the vein and worked its way inside brought a grimace to Gabriella's numb face.

But the warm, tingling sensation as the drug worked its way into her bloodstream raised a sigh of relief from Gabriella's throat. It travelled to the far end of her toes and fingers. Almost immediately, the pain in her side subsided, the dull ache of her huge bruise faded, and her muscles found a new source of life.

Another scream came from the corridor. Heavy pounding like fists on wood. As Gabriella's senses recovered, an image formed of the scene.

A wave of nausea washed over her as she stood, and a rush of blood filled her head with blinding effect. She grasped for the support of a nearby bench, but misjudged her reach and fell to the floor, dizzied.

Climbing to her knees, she rose, slow and steady, controlling the movement, and stepped over to the middle of the room. Through the open rear door of the car in the corridor, she saw Doctor Farrow, enraged and pinning Harvey to the floor. An endless barrage of fists rose and fell, causing dull, hard thumps of bone on bone. Harvey was powerless.

As if sensing her observation, Harvey raised his head. His cold eyes found hers and, for a brief moment, there was an understanding. Then the doctor's fist came down once more and slammed Harvey's head to the floor.

For a second, her body reacted. Her heart began to race. She stepped forward as if she might reach him in time.

But she stopped.

And as the punches rained down on Harvey's body and SFS flowed through her veins bringing a renewed strength to her tired muscles, the darkness outside beckoned.

She whispered a silent thank you to Harvey and stepped outside into the rain.

An electronic buzzer announced the opening of doors followed by a tiny click as the electromagnet locked them into place. Then came a hiss as the air stabilised and finally an extractor kicked into life.

Harvey moved his leg, wincing at the wound that Gabriella had dressed as the dried blood ripped from the material of his pants. His tongue slipped between his lips but found only split skin beneath a layer of dried and crusted blood. Breathing through his nose was close to impossible due to the sharp ends of broken bone that pierced his flesh.

A glass-walled room enclosed Harvey. It was featureless save for the single solid wall with a glass observation window.

Slow footsteps clicked on the linoleum floor.

Harvey opened his eyes, expecting to find himself bound to the gurney he was lying on by ropes or handcuffs. But only the pain in his bruised body stopped him from jumping up and throttling the old man who stepped into view. The man held his hands behind his back with his head upturned as if pondering where to begin.

Kane stared down at Harvey, smiling with inquisitiveness, as a cruel child might when pulling the wings off an insect.

Rolling his neck to one side, Harvey waited for the satisfying click. But his bruised shoulders complained. Even his breathing, which was extremely shallow, hurt like never before.

"Good evening, Mr Stone," said Kane. His voice was clear but dulled by the sound control built into the room.

Harvey didn't reply.

"You're quite the fighter. Most men would have given up with a beating like that. But I am glad you decided to drop by. And I'm glad you decided not to give up on life just yet, Harvey. Can I call you Harvey?" said Kane, leaving no gap for a reply. "You've become quite the thorn in my side."

"You haven't exactly brightened my day, Kane," Harvey mumbled painfully.

"Well, before you get any good ideas, I might remind you that it's feeding time for Doctor Farrow." Kane leaned in closer to Harvey and lowered his voice. Then he opened his hand to reveal a vial of red liquid identical to Gabriella's. "He'll do anything for a fix."

Harvey didn't reply.

"Do you know what this is?" asked Kane, as he stepped over to the glass wall and peered at the wreckage outside.

"I've seen what it does," said Harvey, and gestured at Farrow.

"Why don't we start from the beginning? I'm assuming Miss DuBois put you up to this?" said Kane, ignoring Harvey's flippancy.

Harvey didn't reply. Instead, he locked onto Kane's stare, watching every move, twitch and gesture.

"Would you like something for the pain, Harvey?" said Kane with a smile. "I've got just the thing."

"I don't need anything."

Harvey swung his legs from the gurney and looked around the room.

"Such strength," mused Kane, turning his back to stare back through the glass wall. It was a power move to assure Harvey that Farrow would prevent any attack he was planning. "A man like you would be unstoppable with a little help from me. I could make you rich, you know?"

"I don't want your money," said Harvey, finding his lips dry and his throat scratched with thirst.

"We all have our price, Harvey. There isn't a man I've met in all my years on this earth who wouldn't break his moral code for a fee."

"You haven't met me before."

"My loss, Mr Stone. But I'm sure we'll make up for lost time," said Kane, and offered Harvey a wink in his reflection. "So, where were we? Oh yes. Am I right in assuming that you were coerced into this little enterprise by our friend Miss DuBois?"

"I have nothing to do with her," said Harvey.

"But you do know of her?"

"She broke into my house."

"Your house?" said Kane, feigning ignorance.

"The one you burned down," said Harvey. He felt the jolt of something inside him, like the flicking of a switch as his anger flared, and then subsided.

"I hope you can see how devoted I am to the cause," said Kane. "I've put everything I have into this little enterprise and nothing will stop me now."

"What's the cause?"

"Honour," said Kane, without any hesitation. "Plus, it would be nice to clear my name along the way. It got a little tainted in my younger days. I'd like to leave this world with some kind of legacy, something the world can remember me by, not just my mistakes. You know how it is. People have a tendency to remember the bad and forget about the good."

"Does it matter what other people think?" asked Harvey. A single bead of sweat formed on his brow then began its slow journey down his face before nestling in the two days' growth on his skin.

"I bet you've done some bad things, Mr Stone. I bet there's more to you than meets the eye. The funny thing is, when we searched the databases, Harvey Stone doesn't seem to exist."

"You researched me?" said Harvey, then coughed as burning acid reflux warmed the back of his throat.

"I tried. There's no shame in knowing who you're up against, is there? Know your enemy, Harvey. The first rule of war. Now, in my experience, there are two types of man with your talent and no record. But I can't decide which you are."

Harvey spat on the floor, taking deep breaths and directing his thoughts to an escape.

Kane watched with curiosity, his head cocked to one side and one eye semi-closed, as if he was reading what Harvey was thinking.

"What are my options?" said Harvey. "I'll tell you if you're right."

"Men like you don't exist for a reason. The government keeps you secret. They've invested too much into you. Training. Knowledge. Secrets that will go with you to your grave."

"Or?" asked Harvey.

"Or you're a bad, bad man, Harvey Stone. You've done terrible things that can never be known and you're destined for a life underground. That's why you're out here. That's why you're so upset about your crummy little house. Because it's all you had and all you'll ever have. You so much as raise your head in a crowd and someone out there will take it off, tick a box, and walk away with just another brown envelope. You're a notch on a hit list and nothing more."

Kane allowed a small pause for his two theoretical summaries to digest.

"Why don't *you* tell me which one you are, Harvey? The good news is that I admire both," said Kane. "There's no prejudice here. So, tell me. Who is the *real* Harvey Stone?"

Kane turned back to face the glass wall. His cruel expression softened into a picture of admiration while Harvey took a breath to reply.

"I've got some bad news for you, Kane," said Harvey, as he pushed himself from the gurney and stood for the first time, his bruised bones screaming for some kind of reprise. He found Kane's reflection and fixed his stare. "I'm just a guy who's going to kill the man who burned down his house."

"It's a pity. We would have made a great team," said Kane, with an audible and theatrical sigh. "I suppose Miss DuBois is out to scupper my plans right now, is she?"

"I'd say your plans are well and truly scuppered, Kane," said Harvey.

"How so?" said Kane. "The prime minister is a few hours away, and I still have one man in the field. Plus I'm not too long in the tooth to get my own hands dirty, you know?"

"Who was it Kane?" said Harvey. "Who's paying you?"

"Now, now, Harvey. A good businessman doesn't reveal his sources."

"And what's next? A life on the run?" said Harvey. "Honestly, it's not what it's cracked up to be."

"And why would I run, Harvey?" said Kane. "We'll be heroes."

"If you kill the prime minister, Kane, that's it. You'll have every contract killer in Europe after you, and you can't run forever. They'll hang you by your balls."

"Kill the prime minister?" said Kane, unable to contain a crazed laugh. "Mr Stone, I am not going to kill the prime minister."

"So why are your men placed strategically across the town?" asked Harvey. "Armed to the teeth and preparing for a battle?"

"We're not planning the prime minister's assassination, Mr Stone," said Kane, as he stepped toward Harvey. "We are here to save him."

Harvey didn't reply.

"So where's Gabriella, Harvey?" said Kane, his voice serious and his tone flat and cautious. "I imagine she's comatose somewhere, withdrawal getting the better of her."

"She's gone," said Harvey.

"Gone?" replied Kane, his voice rising as temper reddened his face. "Gone? Do you realise what you've done, you meddling fool?"

Harvey didn't reply.

His thoughts returned to his conversation with Gabriella on the hill, about how Kane was planning the attack, about her military days, and how highly she had spoken of the resistance.

"So it seems your usefulness has expired, Harvey Stone," said Kane, seeing the realisation hit Harvey like a slap in the face. "And my work is still incomplete. So I'll bid you farewell."

Kane moved across to the doorway, where he turned and looked back at Harvey. Then he moved his attention to Farrow.

"You know what to do, Doctor Farrow," said Kane, then pulled the door shut.

Kane appeared on the far side of the glass wall. Harvey limped away from the gurney to face Farrow head on.

But a tiny light appeared in the corner of Harvey's vision.

A flash of steel where Kane was standing.

A flickering orange flame.

And a sickening smile as Kane dropped a lighter into the pool of fuel.

From the rise of the hill in the pouring rain, the fire burned bright against the dark sky and black forest, which filled the valley like a slow moving river in the night.

With one hand on the open door of the SUV, Kane turned and surveyed the sleeping town before him, revising his plan for the prime minister while the citizens counted down the hours to Christmas.

A single road entered the town, dotted with the large villas of the rich until the rows of terraced houses began. Tourist-fuelled restaurants sprawled out from the marina, a catchment for the cruise ships that docked in the port each week.

Obscured by shadows, two alleys sat either side of the road where the terraces began. It had been the perfect place for Bravo team to close the doors. But somewhere in those alleyways, they had been cut down by Stone, leaving the doors wide open.

A distant crack of thunder grew in volume then faded like the grumbling of a bear.

A flash of lightning silenced it; the light formed a snap-shot of the town on Kane's retinas.

At the foot of the main road, the largest rooftop in the small town sprawled from the dockside to the core of the community. All routes led past the fish market. With exits to all corners of the town, it had been the perfect place for an ambush.

But somewhere inside lay the corpses of Alpha team, Kane's best men. His eye twitched at the thought. But the inferno that filled the night behind him satiated his anger.

The entrance to the marina was accessed by two gates at the far end of the town. In his mind's eye, Kane imagined the prime minister and his family with their motorcade driving past the fish market and through the gates. Kane's last man would be scanning the scene through the telescopic scope of his high-powered Diemaco from the church tower.

He raised his radio to his mouth, searching the dark town for the tall steeple.

"Tango-one, this is Charlie-one. Come back."

But only static returned through the radio's tiny speaker. The signal boost from the research facility would be down, and the distance from the hill to the church was too great for the radio waves to travel.

"Tango-one, this is Charlie-one. Come back."

But still, there was no reply.

Climbing back into the car and running his hand through his wet, grey hair, Kane fired the engine into life, killed the lights, and rolled into town, all the while searching the sides of the road for DuBois.

It was just an ordinary night in the alleyways where Bravo team had been stationed. The black SUV, identical to Kane's, was still parked close by. There was no sign of the bodies of his men. Kane stopped the car and searched the alleys.

Tucked into the shadows, Bravo-one stared lifelessly up at the sky, his mouth ajar and frozen with an expression of fear. Bravo-two was lying close by. The rain that pounded his dead flesh was insufficient to wash the blood from his open neck.

Kane examined the bodies and removed all identification. Then he searched the road left and right and tried the radio once more. His proximity to the church was now much closer.

"Tango-one, this is Charlie-one. Come back."

But no reply came.

Kane cruised to the fish market. The five hundred yards required little more than a tickle of the heavy SUV's accelerator. Gravity finished the job, and he rolled to a stop beside the building, leaving the lights on and the engine running.

Heavy rain thundered onto the roof of the long building, drowning out all other sounds save for the low rumble of the storm that hung in the sky above, reluctant to pass by.

The car park was empty, except for the dark corpse that lay on the ground. The body was lit by a flickering light from inside the two sliding doors. Kane stood over Alpha-two and peered into the building. Rows and rows of benches, worn from years of local fishermen selling their catch to tourists and restaurants along the coast, stood proudly in the flickering light.

But at the far end of the space in the loading bay, a grisly form swayed back and forth, hanging lifeless from a block and tackle. A steel hook was buried deep into the back of Alpha-one's head. Strings of blood hung from the body, visible even from afar.

Once more, Kane collected the identification of the men he had served with, the men he had been proud to fight with, and the men with whom he had shared a common disgrace from the country they'd served for most of their adult lives.

He added the IDs to those of Bravo team, and placed them inside his breast pocket. Then he stepped back out into the rain. Three flashes of lightning lit the sky. The first captured Kane's attention. The second allowed him to take in the scene. The third drew his focus to the tallest landmark in the town.

"Tango-one, this is Charlie-one. Come back," said Kane into his radio, half in and half out of the SUV.

Silence.

He stared up at the steeple at the far end of the dockside road, which framed the marina as if holding the town at bay from the welcoming Mediterranean Sea.

"Tango-one, this is Charlie-one. Come back."

He dropped the radio into the inside pocket of the car, climbed in, and closed the door, shutting out the noise of the rain on the fish market roof. The little green LED at the top of the radio lit up. It was faint, but bright enough to catch Kane's eye.

"Charlie-one, I have you in my sights."

Kane froze at the sound of Gabriella's voice. The green LED blinked on once more.

"One wrong move, Monsieur Kane, and I'll put a hole in you big enough to park the prime minister's yacht."

14

HIGH HOPES

"DuBois, you don't know who you're messing with," said Kane over the radio. "You're playing with the big boys now and you're in way over your head."

"Au contraire, Monsieur Kane. I know exactly who you are. I knew about you and your plans even before your imbecile friends captured me. It is you who is ignorant of who *I* am," replied Gabriella. "Do you honestly think that a cretin like Jones could catch me, Gabriella DuBois? I think not."

"Are you trying to tell me you planned on us kidnapping you?" said Kane with a laugh and a single exhale of disbelief. "You could never have known what we were planning."

"Unless we had someone on the inside, Monsieur Kane," said Gabriella. "Someone who had access to all of your plans."

"Would this someone possess the knowledge to create SFS too, Miss DuBois?"

"The knowledge, yes. But alas, we lacked the funds."

A smile, raw and vengeful, found Gabriella's lips as Kane hung his head.

"Farrow was with you all along?" asked Kane.

"You should have done your research, Monsieur Kane.

Farrow was a good friend, as devoted to France as you are devoted to power. But now your power is gone. Your time has passed. In fact, you can count the hours of your remaining life on those stubby little fingers of yours."

She placed the radio resting on the ledge. Positioning herself with her back to the church bell, Gabriella took three deep breaths to control the tingling in her fingers. She flexed her hand then fingered the trigger.

In her sights, the only movement was the wash of wind-blown rain that fell diagonally across the marina.

"I have played your games for long enough. I am no longer your laboratory rat, Monsieur Kane. Now *I* am the master, and you will do everything I say, when I say so."

"You'll die for this, DuBois," said Kane. "No more games. No more small talk. When I'm finished with you, you'll wish you had died in the lab with your dirty little friends, twitching on the ground while their organs failed and their bowels collapsed like the dirty little French whores there were."

A rush of blood dizzied Gabriella. It was enough to elicit a smile but faint enough for her to bring it under control with a few breaths of the cold air. It was too early to peak.

"And who will do such a thing?" said Gabriella. "Your men are all dead. All that remains of Kane's Army is a sad, pathetic old man."

"It isn't over yet, DuBois."

"No," said Gabriella. "No, you're right. In one hour, the sun will rise, and the prime minister and his motorcade will drive into Saint-Pierre, safe in the knowledge that Kane's Army has secured the town."

She paused, giving Kane time to imagine what was in store for him.

"In two hours, you will be dead," said Gabriella. "But in the eyes of the French people, you will be a hero. If I were you, I would let that little thought carry you through to the morning."

"We have a very different understanding of the word hero, DuBois."

"Remove the keys from the ignition," said Gabriella, maintaining control of the situation. "Try to run and I'll cut you down."

The interior light of the SUV flashed on. Kane stepped out into the rain, closing the door behind him. He stared up at the church tower.

Through the rifle scope, Gabriella met his stare. The cross-hairs met in the centre of his chest. She adjusted her aim, finding his forehead. She imagined pulling the trigger. The spray of red mist. His body as it crumpled to the ground.

Kane raised the radio to his mouth. "Now what?"

Gabriella returned the rifle to aim at his chest, the largest target with the most devastating result.

"Toss the keys into the boat yard," replied Gabriella. She watched him throw the keys, keeping sight on him at all times. "Are you armed, Monsieur Kane?"

"You can see me. Why don't you tell me?" replied Kane.

"You have a handgun under your jacket on your left side. Remove the gun."

Kane did as requested. As any man with military experience might, he felt the weight of his handgun with a practiced hand.

"How many rounds?" asked Gabriella.

Kane looked up at the church again as if he was surprised that she saw the movement.

"A full magazine," he replied.

"Good," said Gabriella. "Although you will need only one."

"You're running out of time, Gabriella."

"Au contraire, Monsieur Kane. It is you who is running out of time," said Gabriella, enjoying the power she held over the man who threatened everything for which she had lived. "Kneel on the ground."

Even from a thousand yards, Kane's outrage was clear. He stared up at her with his arms outstretched as if questioning her sanity.

"Do it, Monsieur Kane."

"You're out of your mind, Gabriella. There is no more time for games."

Adjusting her aim to the right, Gabriella fired once. The headlight of the car smashed. She returned her aim to Kane.

"Next time it's your knee," said Gabriella. "Now kneel."

Kane bent one leg, held onto the wet ground for stability, and then bent his other leg and knelt on the hard concrete.

"Is this it?" said Kane. "Is this how I die?"

"No, Monsieur Kane. This is how you repent. Close your eyes and turn your face to the rain."

The distance was too far to see, but with his face upturned to the skies, Gabriella assumed that Kane's eyes were closed.

"Now, Monsieur Kane, put the gun to your head."

There was no movement for a second, save for the cocking of Kane's head to one side as he struggled to comprehend the instruction.

"You heard me correctly," said Gabriella. "Place the gun to your head."

Kane did as requested.

"Repeat these words after me," said Gabriella, her voice calm. She closed her eyes and gave thought to those that had fallen in the battle, grateful to reach the end.

"Claudia Deseille," said Gabriella.

No reply came.

"I have only one headlight left, Monsieur Kane. Do I need to fire another warning shot?"

"Claudia Deseille," spat Kane, then lowered the radio.

"Monica Deux," said Gabriella.

"Monica Deux," said Kane. He exhaled the words as if he understood what Gabriella was trying to do and felt that the recital was needless.

"Estella Bouchard," said Gabriella.

"Estella Bouchard."

Pausing to allow Kane to reflect on the names he'd recited, Gabriella opened her eyes and found him in her sight. He was ready to die. He had accepted death long before he'd stepped foot on a battle field.

"Donna Almeida," said Gabriella.

She felt the pang of SFS release into her blood like a hot coffee on cold teeth.

Kane remained silent, as if saying the name and reaching the end of the recital would instigate his end.

"Monsieur Kane, say her name," said Gabriella. "Donna Almeida."

"Donna Almeida," said Kane. The voice cracked from interference over the radio and the broken tones of a guilty man. He straightened his posture, kneeling tall and proud, waiting for the bullet.

A tear formed in Gabriella's eye and she cleared her throat of emotion, holding the push-to-talk button down on the radio, but saying nothing.

The one movement she allowed him was to hang his head in shame.

"Thank you, Monsieur Kane," said Gabriella. "Are you ready to die for your honour?"

***

The lack of airflow in the glass-walled room combined with the fire that raged in the corridor outside encouraged a layer of sweat on Harvey's skin that soaked into his clothes.

Farrow slid down the rear wall to the floor. All anger and aggression for Harvey had dissipated, leaving just the shell of a drug-fuelled man whose body had entered into self-destruction.

Tall flames licked at the corridor ceiling, angry and unrelenting in their efforts to chew through anything that stood in their path, demonstrating to Harvey and Farrow what lay in store for them when the glass gave way.

"How long will it last?" said Harvey.

He paced along the length of the glass and stood beside the control room window. The control room still sat in relative peace and darkness, its conditions untainted by the blaze of orange that crept along the corridor outside.

Farrow stared back at him, offering an expression that conveyed an acceptance of death.

"Can you talk?" asked Harvey. But Farrow slumped further, his broken mind and dying body clinging to the cool wall. "Farrow," said Harvey, crouching before him, "we have to get out of here."

Farrow stared back at him. He raised a hand and touched Harvey's swollen face as if ashamed of what he had done. His red eyes moistened and a tear formed in the corner of each eye.

Farrow shook his head then turned his face against the wall.

"Farrow, how long will the air last?" said Harvey, grabbing Farrow's shoulders and losing control of his anger.

The aggression roused the forlorn man from his semi-slumber. He flinched at the touch of Harvey's hand and, in an instant, gripped him by the neck, holding with an iron-like grip despite Harvey's attempts to break free.

Climbing to his feet, Farrow dragged Harvey up and across the floor to the control room window, where he slammed him into the glass.

"Don't you see?" said Farrow, with more of a breath than articulated words. "We both die here."

Harvey pulled at the man's hands with everything he had, but to no avail. The grip seemed to strengthen with Harvey's efforts.

"I'm dying," said Farrow. "I can feel my body failing."

"There's time to get out," gasped Harvey. "There's time to get Kane."

"Die with me here before the fire consumes us both," said Farrow, as if his offer of death was some sort of compensation for the beating he'd given Harvey.

"Stop, Farrow," said Harvey, struggling to suck in the thinning air. "Don't do this."

But Farrow increased the strength of his grip, pinching at Harvey's windpipe and slamming him into the glass.

With only seconds of strength left, Harvey began an onslaught of punches.

But no matter how hard Harvey punched and kicked, the blows failed to halt Farrow's efforts. He slammed Harvey into the wall, pressing his face against the control room window.

Harvey's hands fumbled for Farrow's face. His thumbs found the soft eye sockets and forced an entry, pushing the eyeballs back until Farrow screamed and squeezed Harvey's throat, closing off whatever gap remained.

Deeper and deeper, Harvey forced his thumbs inside the sockets. He pulled at the sinew inside, finding taut nerves that seemed to electrify Farrow. But still, the man held onto Harvey's neck. A thick sweat glazed Farrow's skin. As the two men grappled, each of them pushing the other closer to death, bright lights danced in Harvey's vision. A darkness enveloped his sight and the beat of his dying heart thumped like a bass drum inside his chest.

Without warning, a pane of the glass wall exploded from the heat and vacuum of air.

Angry flames licked at the walls around them both, searching for fuel. They found Farrow's tortured body.

He screamed and released Harvey, who pulled his hands back to cover his face from the searing heat. Harvey fell to the floor, gasping for air. His fingers searched for something to grip on the smooth linoleum floor to pull himself away and find somewhere cooler.

The flames receded, finding no air to fuel its rage, and the next pane of glass cracked from top to bottom as the heat overwhelmed the glass.

Harvey dragged himself to his feet, his raspy breath sucking in as much air as it could. He pulled one of the big heavy gurneys closer then lifted it, holding it high above his head. Then he hurled it at the control room window.

Nothing happened. The gurney bounced back and fell to the floor at his feet.

Then the glass partition became a wall of raging flames as the fire closed in, trying to enter the control room. Inside, the ceiling had begun to smoulder and thick smoke rolled through the top of the doorway.

Seeing his last chance of escape become engulfed in flames, Harvey pulled the gurney up above his head once more, stepped back, and smashed it into the window with everything he had.

Nothing happened. His attempts were too weak to scratch the glass. He struck the glass three more times. But the oxygen in the air had grown too thin. Harvey dizzied. He rested the end of the gurney on the floor, leaning his weight on it while sucking in empty air.

Through the control room window, flickering orange crept into view, finding new fuel in the untouched walls and ceiling.

Harvey dropped to one knee, unable to hold his own weight.

A hand gripped Harvey's shoulder.

Instinct sent the signal to his brain to defend himself and strike out, but his body was starved of oxygen. He let go of the frame and braced for the final blow that would finish him.

But no blow came.

The gurney was wrenched from Harvey's grip. He toppled and fell to the floor. The bright lights that had danced across his vision in wondrous circles now succumbed to the darkness that was closing in. The pain in his chest, likes stabs of a blade, grew stronger as his lungs sought fresh, clean air but found only thick, black smoke.

The next partition of the glass wall shattered. The flames erupted as if rejoicing at their invasion and reached out across the ceiling.

The control room window was framed with a mix of fiery reds and oranges. Harvey turned his face to the floor, seeking a layer of air as the room prepared to collapse.

Harvey closed his eyes.

Another bang sounded, louder than the first. Glass shattered behind him as more of the glass wall gave in, and a rush of heat filled the room, fighting for the same sparse oxygen as Harvey.

Farrow screamed, wild and angry. The yell evolved into a growl that culminated in a final smash of glass. Harvey rolled, peering through one eye in time to see the gurney disappearing through the control room window.

A hand, strong but gentle, pulled at Harvey's arm. He tried to fight back, but there was nothing left. Even as Farrow pulled him to his feet and lifted him, Harvey's fingers searched for a weakness, the eye, the ears, anything.

A breeze touched Harvey's face. It was weak, but it was there, fractions of a degree cooler than the hot air that was suffocating him. He opened his eyes as Farrow held him up to the window, trying to pass him through the gap into the control room.

Hope reared its head.

He sensed a taste of oxygen, faint, but enough to tease Harvey's dying body.

But as Farrow leaned through the hole, pushing Harvey to safety, the ceiling above them collapsed. Burning timber and ceiling fixtures dropped into the room, landing on Harvey and Farrow, and pinning Harvey to the ground with its burning dead weight. Intense heat singed Harvey's face and hands. Smoke stung at his eyes like hot sand. There was nowhere to turn, no refuge from the blaze.

With a roar of sheer power and animal strength, Farrow threw himself through the flames and fell to the floor. He pulled the burning debris off Harvey, who rolled to his knees and clambered back to the one remaining wall that wasn't ablaze.

Harvey pushed himself to his feet and shielded his face from the intense heat. But through the flickering flames and heat haze, he saw Farrow crouching in the collapsed doorway. The man who had been so close to death just ten minutes before, whose body had entered into self-destruction mode, began to stand.

The timbers across his back found skin with a hiss that was audible above the crackling destruction of wood. He growled once more. It wasn't a roar of anger. It wasn't a cry of pain. It was the final growl of a man who was sacrificing his life in repent.

Timbers fell around him, scorching his melting skin. His hair took flame and lit his anguished face. But he rose to full height, creating a small gap in the flaming debris for Harvey to escape.

As the flames danced across Farrow's ruined face, his

pain-filled stare found Harvey's eyes. No words were needed. There was no time for sorrow.

"Now," Farrow cried.

He squeezed his burning eyes closed and let out one final scream of spent energy and frustration.

With just fractions of a second to spare, Harvey threw himself between Farrow's legs into the corridor. He rolled to where the fire had yet to reach. A cool stretch of linoleum lay beneath a layer of cool oxygen.

Harvey rolled to his feet and reached into the fire, fumbling to pull Farrow free.

But it was too late.

As Harvey's outstretched hand touched Farrow's melting skin, the rest of the control room ceiling and walls gave way. Harvey leaped for the safety of the unburned stretch of corridor. He turned to witness a frenzy of flames rush across the debris pile in a victorious dance of orange and red with Farrow beneath it, his sins repented.

"How does it feel?" said Gabriella over the radio.

Kane sighed and hit the push-to-talk button. "Do you think this is the first time I've had a gun pointed at me?"

"A man like you? No. I imagine there have been many men who have had you in their sights," said Gabriella. "But rest assured, this will be the last."

"And if I pulled the trigger now? What would you do then?"

"I would do nothing. My plan would continue and you would die, shamed, as you are now," said Gabriella. "Don't you see, Monsieur Kane? I am offering you a chance to redeem yourself, to clear your name. I am offering you a chance to save France and all she stands for."

"Why would I care about France?"

"You would be a hero. I've seen how you wear those medals on your chest, regardless of your disgrace. You have no honour. Men like you seek glory whatever the cost."

"You don't know anything about me, Gabriella," said Kane. "You were just a lab rat, a disposable lump of meat in the palm of my hand."

"Lower the weapon, Monsieur Kane."

Kane glanced up at the tower in the distance.

"I said lower it," said Gabriella.

He lowered the gun.

"Now get up and walk."

"Where am I walking?"

"To victory, Monsieur Kane," said Gabriella. "When the prime minister arrives, you will be standing there waiting for him. He will see you, so he can recognise your infinite leadership skills and the quality of Kane's Army."

Kane said nothing. He just stared up at the church tower.

"But your success will be short-lived. You will die. But whether you die a hero or the disgraced fool you are is up to you," said Gabriella. "Now walk."

Kane began the long walk, following the path the prime minister's small motorcade would be taking in the morning. He splashed through puddles of rain water and considered his defeat. What would it mean to the men that had died for him? Killed while fighting for their names to be freed from their tarnished state. Failure now would seal their fate.

"Are you going to tell me how you pulled this off?" said Kane. "Surely now is the time to gloat."

"We've known about your plans for some time," said Gabriella. "We have spies everywhere and we are all willing to die for France."

"All of you?" said Kane. The statement invoked a

conscious thought that held the faces of his men at bay. "Who's all of you?"

"Donna," said Gabriella, "Claudia, Monica, Estella. We were all against you. There are others, as I'm sure you will know. We are willing to die for our beloved France. Not even the vile tactics of a disgraced British military officer could stop us."

"So it's true," said Kane. "You are resistance."

"Yes. If you have to categorise us, if your analytical mind must place us, then we are the French Resistance. Too long have we hidden in the shadows. To long have we been forced underground. We fight for France. We fight for everything she stands for."

"I don't see any others," said Kane. "Does the future of France rest on the whims of one stupid girl and her idiotic fantasies about right and wrong?"

Gabriella laughed, admiring Kane's confident officer-like gait from afar.

"The prime minister will be here in thirty minutes," she said. "He will arrive unannounced to spend a private Christmas with his family in his yacht. It is the perfect opportunity for an assassination. Am I right, Monsieur Kane?"

"Yes," said Kane.

"The French government knows this. But to install a security detail would bring too much attention to this small town. Would it not, Monsieur Kane?" said Gabriella. "People would talk. They would wonder why the military walked their streets. The prime minister's visit would be all over the national newspapers. It would be an invitation for many nationalists to come and vent their anger at the man who is bringing France to its knees."

"People often pay no attention to what is in front of their faces, DuBois," said Kane.

"And that is why Kane's Army were hired, a team of highly trained men who can patrol the streets without raising an eyelid. Am I correct, Monsieur Kane?"

"That's about the size of it," said Kane. "Is there a point to all of this?"

"So let me finish my summary," said Gabriella. "Let me explain what this stupid girl and her idiotic whims of what is right and wrong has accomplished. Behind you, at the entrance to town, is the perfect place for Bravo team to secure the town of Saint-Pierre. No escape. Am I right, Monsieur Kane?"

"Yes."

"And the fish market beside you is the perfect place for an ambush, so it must be guarded. I'm sure you found Alpha team by now."

"Yes," said Kane, remembering the hook in the back of Alpha-one's head.

He crossed the street with the dockside on his left and the church ahead on the right overlooking the small town.

"And from the church tower of Saint-Pierre, Tango team can see the whole town. He was your last resort, was he not, Monsieur Kane?"

"Yes," said Kane. "So what?"

"So now, when the prime minister drives into the town, there will be no Bravo team to lock the doors behind him. There is no Alpha team to prevent an ambush. And there is no Tango team to overlook the town. There is just you, me, and the prime minister, Monsieur Kane."

"Why are you doing this, DuBois?" said Kane.

"For my love of France. For freedom and for revenge," said Gabriella. "We will both be heroes. The only difference is that I'll be alive to enjoy my glory."

Kane stopped at the edge of the dockside. Dark, inky water lapped against the concrete. The Mediterranean Sea beyond the port was pale with white caps merging in the wind. The rows of vessels, from small fishing boats to sailing yachts, rocked back and forth with the ebb and flow of the storm-driven water.

"So how is this going to work?" said Kane.

"The best plans are always the simplest, Monsieur Kane. The plan differs from your own only in the final act. You will wait where you are. The prime minister will arrive and you will be greeted. You will be thanked and complimented on the excellent security, leaving you to escort him and his family to his yacht."

"I'm gaining his trust?" said Kane.

"Yes, Monsieur Kane. The prime minister will allow his family to board the yacht. His staff will carry their bags and the prime minister will board the boat last. The moment he turns his back, you will fire a single shot into the back of his head. Your name will forever be tarnished in the eyes of the military. But, Monsieur Kane, in the eyes of France, you will be a hero."

"And if I don't?" said Kane, with an exhale. "If I don't pull the trigger?"

"Ah, Monsieur Kane," said Gabriella. "If you do not kill the prime minister, the consequences for you will be beyond your wildest imagination."

15

STAIRWAY TO HEAVEN

THREE PAIRS OF HEADLIGHTS APPEARED AT BRAVO checkpoint. They passed by unhindered and cruised into the town. Bravo team did not close in behind them.

The first and last cars were both police Peugeots. The middle car was a sleek, black saloon. The motorcade continued down the hill to the fish market, which they passed without incident. Alpha team were not surveilling the area for an attack.

The cars drove on, washing through a long rain puddle, maintaining the thirty-kilometres-per-hour speed limit despite having one of France's most prominent targets on board, despite the town being deserted on Christmas Eve, and despite the apparent lack of security.

The three cars pulled into the marina, took a wide half-circle and stopped beside the yacht's boardwalk, where Kane was standing to attention.

"It is show time, Monsieur Kane," said Gabriella.

The two policemen in the first car remained seated, but the passenger door of the saloon opened and a man in a suit appeared. He glanced around at the empty space and nodded at Kane before approaching him.

"I have your eyeball in my cross-hairs, Monsieur Kane," said Gabriella. "If you try anything stupid, you will die a failure and a disgrace. Blink twice if you understand."

Kane blinked twice then offered his hand to the prime minister's chief of security.

"Mr Kane?" said the man.

"Good morning, Monsieur Berger," replied Kane.

"The area is secure? I haven't been able to reach you. We agreed on open communications, did we not?"

Kane nodded. "Apologies, Monsieur Berger. It must be the storm." Kane waved his hand at the sky then opened his palm out to catch a few drops of rain. "It's been playing up all night."

Berger studied Kane as if reading him with a trained eye.

"Is everything okay, Monsieur Kane?" asked Berger. "You seem a little distracted."

"I'm fine," said Kane. "It's been a long night, that's all."

"And your men? Where are your men? You promised me a minimum of three teams. Yet nobody stopped us on the way into town. I saw no men at the agreed check point. Where are they, Monsieur Kane?"

"I promised you security, Mr Berger. That you cannot see my men is a testament to their skills."

"Very good, Monsieur Kane," said Berger, offering a nod with a hint of suspicion. "Is there anything I should know? Were there any incidents at all?"

Berger continued to examine Kane, waiting for an answer. But Kane remained silent.

"Monsieur Kane. I asked you a question," said Berger. "Is there anything I should know about?"

"Charlie-one, this is Tango-two," said Gabriella through the radio. "All clear, sir. Nothing to report."

Through the scope, Gabriella saw Berger raising his eyebrows.

"Nothing to report, then?" said Berger.

"Nothing to report," said Kane, snapping out of his daze.

The two men met in a stare. Berger's inquisitive eyes searched for a hint of disbelief. Kane's blank stare offered nothing in response but a seed of doubt and a flavour of fear.

"Very well, Monsieur Kane. Let's get this over with," said Berger.

He turned, gave the small marina a thorough visual examination then stepped over to the saloon and opened the rear door. He retrieved a black umbrella from the parcel shelf and popped it open in time for a tall man in a casual sports jacket, cream pants and boat shoes to step out. The prime minister buttoned his jacket, collected the umbrella from Berger, and held out his hand for his family to follow. A small boy climbed outside then turned and waited for his mother, displaying the mannerisms of a well-educated young man rather than the average boy who might have run to the gangway and onto the boat.

The first lady of France followed, her smile barely weakened by the harsh wind and incessant rain. She stood beside her husband, who passed her the umbrella, then she took the boy's hand. The prime minister extended his arm, allowing his wife and son to board the yacht. Then, as two staff carried two cases aboard, he shook Berger's hand. He turned to board the boat but stopped when he saw Kane. His eyes flicked between the two men as if requesting an answer to an unspoken question.

"Sir, may I introduce Monsieur Kane," said Berger, his voice hinting at a bitterness or reluctance to make the introduction.

"Keep your cool, Monsieur Kane," whispered Gabriella.

"Anglais?" said the prime minister.

"Yes, sir," replied Kane.

The prime minister offered his hand to Kane, who hesitated, then reached out and shook it.

"Our journey was uneventful. I believe we have you to thank, Monsieur Kane," said the prime minister. "We were expecting the journey to be a little bumpy."

"Enjoy your Christmas, sir," replied Kane, and offered him a weak smile.

The prime minister nodded. "And you," he replied. Then he nodded his approval at Berger and turned to board the boat.

"Are you ready, Monsieur Kane?" whispered Gabriella. "Glory and honour await."

"Sorry, sir?" said Kane as the prime minister placed his foot on the gangway.

He turned to face Kane, his hand on the rail.

"Now," said Gabriella.

"There is just one more thing," said Kane.

He raised his weapon as Gabriella's first shot entered the side of Berger's head.

A single shot sang out in the night. It came from a high powered rifle from the church steeple above where Harvey stood with his hand on the ancient door handle.

The incessant wind that tore into Saint-Pierre from the sea bit into the burns on his face, but eased when the cool church air touched his skin. At the east end of the church was a door either side of a raised platform, where Harvey assumed a choir would stand. The door to the left had been built into the curved, stone wall. The tower rose above it, disappearing into the vaulted ceiling and beyond.

The tiny echoes of Harvey's boots seemed to wake a thousand years of memories that whispered in the shadows, the eaves and the galleys. He stopped at the wooden pew closest to the chancel and, for the first time in his life, he sat down in a church.

There was no lowering of his head in prayer or thoughts of those he had loved. Just a rare peace. A peace he had sought for too long.

No thoughts of God crossed Harvey's mind as he marvelled at the stories told by the stained windows. But he felt a curious understanding, perhaps more than ever before, about the solace others found in prayer.

The space held a thousand years of births and deaths, weekly prayers, and sorrowful confessions, and there Harvey sat for the tiniest fraction of time. Another thousand years of births and deaths would follow, although they would be stained by the violence Harvey was about to bring to the peace.

An apology formed on Harvey's lips, as soundless as it was subconscious and prominent in his mind. The memories that stared down at him from the lofty shadows of the vaulted ceiling seemed tangible. It was as if he could touch them, or if he spoke, be heard by them.

Or be seen by them. His actions might be judged by the presence of peace itself.

Shadows buried the aisles to each side of the nave and concealed Harvey's approach. But still, the eyes of memories bore into him, teasing his conscience with reminders of the purity he was about to taint with the blood of man.

He stopped at the door to the tower with his hand against the wood. Something was watching him, something more than the memories of happiness and peace that filled the ancient space. Eyes drilled into him. Unafraid.

Lowering his hand, Harvey remained still, his senses alive in his new surroundings.

As if acknowledging Harvey's awareness of his presence, a figure, robed and silent, stepped from the darkness with the confidence of a man who knew no fear and held the greatest power in his heart.

In a silent exchange of questioning expressions, the priest conveyed an understanding of Harvey's purpose. He nodded. The movement of his head was almost imperceptible in the dark church. Only the motion of the glints of his eyes were clear.

Harvey turned the ancient handle and pulled the door, which opened with surprising ease. No creaks or groans broke the silence. Only the first cold, stone steps of a narrow curved staircase presented itself before the priest spoke. His voice was old and cracked like the ancient timbers that sheltered them both from the storm.

"Prenez la mort de cet endroit," said the priest.

"Anglais?" replied Harvey in a whisper, finding his throat parched and his own voice cracked.

Long robes fell over the priest's feet as he moved closer to stand in front of Harvey, fearless with his God by his side. He reached out a folded arm, the long sleeves unfurling to reveal a thin, weak hand that rested on Harvey's shoulder.

"Take death from this place."

The staircase, narrow and curved, led clockwise with walls that threatened to squeeze Harvey the further up he climbed. It was as if the church itself knew that death had crossed its threshold. He turned sideways, taking soft steps and listening for a sign.

Narrow windows, empty of glass and as wide as Harvey's fist, adorned the baron walls with each sweeping turn. One was home to a pair of pigeons, who neither saw nor heard Harvey approach or move past them as they perched on the ledge, their heads buried in plumes of thick feathers.

At the top of the staircase, the dim, morning light

revealed an old wooden door, framed by a stone arch no higher than Harvey's shoulders, and much narrower.

A soft tuneful murmur came from the far side of the door. It was the hum of a song that sounded familiar, along with the aroma of one-thousand-year-old stone and dust.

Harvey lay his hand against the painted wood and closed his eyes, picturing the scene on the far side of the door.

The image in Harvey's mind showed a bell hanging from the centre with a narrow walkway around the edge. There would be large open windows below the pitched roof offering a three-hundred-and-sixty-degree view of Saint-Pierre.

The sweet, tuneful humming had ceased and a silence ensued that offered Harvey small teases of the tiniest movements.

"Are you ready, Monsieur Kane?" said Gabriella.

Harvey ran his finger along the grain in the wood, his eyes closed, picturing the scene. In his mind, he placed Gabriella to the left, her back to the door and her focus on Kane.

A strong wind touched his burned face with the hint of a sting. But it also allowed him to orient his position in relation to the sea.

"Now," said Gabriella.

A spray of red mist covered Kane's face. He spat the iron taste from his lips, holding the prime minister in his sights along the length of his handgun.

The police cars burst into life. All four doors opened and all four policemen began to wave their guns, searching the boat yard for the source of the shot.

The second shot burst through the chest of the policeman closest to the prime minister.

The prime minister froze to the spot. His eyes were wide,

his mouth hung open and his legs shook as he was unable to hold himself still.

"Tell the prime minister to step off the boat, Monsieur Kane," said Gabriella over the radio.

"Step away from the boat, sir," said Kane.

The remaining three cops turned their guns on him.

Gabriella fired another round that severed the neck of the lead cop. He dropped to his knees, choking on his own blood.

"Toss the guns into the water," said Kane. "Or the prime minister is next."

Two splashes confirmed the policemen had obeyed the order.

"You're making a big mistake," said the prime minister. "I'll see that you die for this, Kane."

"Please, sir, step off the boat."

"I knew we couldn't trust a bunch of hired guns," the prime minister continued, as he stepped away from the boat. "You will die for this."

Kane gestured with his weapon for the prime minister to move past the cars and into the open ground where, he knew, DuBois would be able to see him through her scope. But in the distance, above the wind and the rain, the sound of approaching stomping feet began to grow louder.

"Remove your headset, Kane," said Gabriella. "I wish to talk with the prime minister."

Kane did as instructed, pulling the cable from the radio and tossing it to the ground, then he held out the radio. But the prime minister was transfixed on the sight of a hundred or more people marching in unison toward the marina. The dark shape of their mass and the volume of their boots formed a terrifying image. The policemen began to step back towards the water's edge, their worried faces a picture of fear and uncertainty.

"Monsieur Prime Minister," said Gabriella. Her voice

sounded tinny through the small speaker, but her confidence carried through despite the incessant wind that blew off the sea in a growing rage and rocked the smaller boats moored in the marina. "You will, no doubt, be questioning your decision to employ the services of Monsieur Kane. And you would be correct to do so."

The prime minister turned to look at his yacht. Through a small port hole, he saw his wife staring down at him and holding her son close with a look of terror on her face.

The mass of people stopped at the gates of the marina, blocking the exit. A single man's voice began to chant. The crowd replied with audible anger.

"Monsieur Prime Minister, do I have your attention?" said Gabriella.

Kane held the push-to-talk button down for the prime minister to reply.

"You have my attention. Who am I talking to?" said the prime minister, shouting to be heard above the chanting crowd one hundred yards away.

"My name is Gabriella DuBois, Monsieur Prime Minister."

The prime minister's eyes flicked from the yacht to the mass of people at the marina gates, and then to Kane.

"You are Gabriella DuBois, sister of Francis DuBois? The infamous leader of the French rebellion? He was a traitor to France."

"My brother was not a traitor, Prime Minister. He was a patriot. He died for what he believed in, and his blood has stained your hands for long enough."

"He was a traitor, DuBois," said the prime minister. "He died because he was a threat to France and all we stand for. You and all these people, is this it? Is this the sum total of your so-called rebellion?"

"We prefer to call ourselves La Resistance," said Gabriella. "And we are many, many more than what you see."

"The resistance died with World War Two, DuBois. The resistance had honour. They fought for the nation and its people."

"You're correct, Monsieur Prime Minister. Look at the crowds in front of you. They are the people. It is they who suffer at your hands. We fight for our nation. Only this time, instead of ridding France of its Nazi occupation, we are disposing of the corrupt, selfish government. The time for change is long overdue. The time for action is now. If you want your family to survive, you will do everything I say. Do I make myself clear?"

"My family?" said the prime minister. "Leave them out of this, Miss DuBois."

"I will try my hardest, Prime Minister. But do you see my friends at the gates? They are angry. Something must be done to save this country from the turmoil you have created. A new government must be empowered, a government that recognises France and *all* its people as great, not just the wealthy minority. A new balance must be found, and for that to happen, I am afraid, you must die."

As if on cue, a rumble of thunder rolled across the sky. Two great flashes of lightning lit the marina and the mass of angry rebels who waited at the gates.

"Monsieur Kane, I am now talking to you. I have you in my cross-hairs," said Gabriella. "It is time."

Kane sighed and hung his head. Rain fell from his nose and chin. For the first time, his boots felt like lead weights, gripped by fear and indecision. He stared back at the church tower.

"Monsieur Kane, I will explain. The prime minister and you have two options. Are you hearing me? Do you under-stand? Tell me you understand, Monsieur Kane."

He raised the radio to his mouth, hit the push-to-talk button and spoke through his choked throat. "I understand, DuBois."

"Option one," said Gabriella. "You will raise your weapon to the prime minister's head and pull the trigger. The crowd before you will rush in and raise you up. You will be a hero. You will be on the front page of every newspaper across the world."

Kane's stomach rolled. He blinked away the rain drops that disguised his tears.

"And option two?" said Kane.

"You fail to kill the prime minister. The resistance will storm the marina and may God help anybody who stands in their way."

16

THE GREAT GIG IN THE SKY

Standing from her position behind the tower wall, Gabriella rose and outstretched her arms. The resistance could see her figure in the dim morning light. Her crowd roared in response, and the chanting began again with renewed vigour, awaiting her command.

She held out her hand, palm facing out, and the crowd below faded to silence. Only the hissing of rain hitting the ground and the rushing of wind off the sea could be heard.

"The fate of the prime minister's family resides with you, Monsieur Kane," said Gabriella over the radio. "It is time to decide."

Below, standing in the centre of the marina with the Mediterranean Sea behind him and a hundred rebels in front, hungry for blood, Kane raised his weapon and aimed at the prime minister's head.

A woman's scream cried out from inside the yacht. It was carried by the wind to Gabriella's ears, raising a smile on her tired face. She lifted the rifle to her shoulder and found Kane in the scope, his head a perfect fit between the cross-hairs.

Kane mouthed an apology to the prime minister, who

dropped to his knees with his hands behind his head. But he remained resolute with a straight back, a proud man who would die for his family and stare at his killer with open eyes.

"Now, Monsieur Kane," said Gabriella, "or I will order the attack."

But Kane's hand began to shake. He supported the weight of the weapon with his left hand, but still, the muzzle wavered.

The angry crowd tensed. The atmosphere was electric amongst the rain-soaked bodies who fought their way to the front of the group to be the first to get their hands on the man who was destroying their country.

"Now, Kane," screamed Gabriella.

But Kane lowered the weapon.

He stood staring wide-eyed at the prime minister, who was shouting at him to pull the trigger, to save his family.

Kane shook his head.

He dropped the weapon to the ground.

The prime minister glanced back at his family.

And Gabriella gave the signal for the charge.

A surge of people stormed through the gates of the marina. Their chants turned to battle cries. The rhythmic stomping of their feet, which had percussed the initial negotiations, gave way to a flood of heavy boots that charged at the prime minister and Kane.

"May God be with you all," said Gabriella, and lowered the radio as a wave of bodies engulfed the two men.

Gabriella lowered the rifle to the floor of the tower.

Harvey stepped up behind her.

"For you, my brother," she whispered.

But her sentiment was lost to sudden confusion as, from

nowhere, bright spot lights lit the riot on the ground below. She searched the skies for the source of the lights as a familiar sound became clear, carried to the church tower during a brief lull in the wind.

The scene below grew brighter. Then, to Gabriella's despair, two military helicopters shot past either side of the church tower, banking hard to come to a hover above the rioting crowd.

Cries of anger rose up from the battle below and the fighting intensified.

"No," screamed Gabriella, leaning from the tower into the wind and the rain. "Finish them."

The side doors of the choppers opened and two ropes dropped from both helicopters.

Gabriella fumbled for the rifle behind her, but found nothing.

She turned to look and pressed her neck into the blade of Harvey's waiting knife. But before he could react, she arched backward, rolled, and sprung to her feet.

"Monsieur Stone, you're just in time for the fun," said Gabriella, keeping the huge church bell between them.

Keeping Gabriella in sight, Harvey followed her around the bell, the narrow walkway no wider than the length of his boots.

Below the bell, a pitch-dark chasm fell to the depths of the church. Behind Harvey was a drop to the ground of Saint-Pierre, where the cobbled streets below would break every bone in his body.

But Gabriella moved with feline grace, stepping forward then back, taunting Harvey and laughing at his clumsy attempts to follow her.

With his free hand, he tossed the rifle from the tower, where it landed without a sound on the street below.

"I can't let you do this, Gabriella," said Harvey. "You lied to me."

"You would never have helped me if you had known the truth, Harvey," replied Gabriella, backing away around the narrow circular walkway.

Matching her step for step, Harvey followed her, watching her feet below the rim of the bell.

He shoved at the giant bell, but the weight was too great and the swing too slow to make an impact. The deafening chime of the huge, hollow bronze filled the tiny space and Gabriella's feet danced to one side.

Harvey lurched to grab her, but she slipped away as the bell receded. He followed, using the short dwarf wall to stop him from falling over the edge. But Gabriella was too fast and nimble.

Using the momentum of the bell, she forced it toward him on the return swing. Harvey dove to the stone floor as the bell swung over him. He searched the walkway opposite for Gabriella as the swinging bell sang its song, loud and proud for the entire town to hear.

But she wasn't there.

He jumped to his feet, sidestepped the deafening bell once more, and edged around the walkway.

But there was no sign of her.

Behind him, a helicopter turned its spotlights on the church tower and banked towards them.

"The fun's over, Gabriella," said Harvey. "You can't escape from this."

A short burst of automatic fire caused a series of tiny explosions in the church's stonework. Harvey dropped to the floor once more as the gunfire tore into the wall behind him. He peered over the parapet wall to find a man in military fatigues preparing for another burst.

The helicopter banked as the pilot sought a new angle,

but as Harvey stood, Gabriella swung from the rafters above. Her feet caught him square in the face, forcing him backward into the low parapet wall.

Gabriella dropped to the floor in front of him and began an onslaught of punches that connected with Harvey's already bruised body, never landing in the same place twice. The first rocked his head to one side. The second caught his solar plexus, winding him. He bent forward, sucking in air as the third blow, an uppercut, sent him reeling backwards.

The reprise allowed him time to block the next round of punches. Seeing a gap in Gabriella's attack, he lurched forward and smashed his forehead into her face.

She spat blood from her mouth, and smiled as the down-draft from the rotor blades ripped at her clothes and sent her hair waving in all directions. As the gunman opened fire once more, she ran at Harvey. Her shoulder slammed into his gut and her feet scrambled on the stone floor for purchase, forcing him back further and further until there was no more walkway and the back of his legs found the low parapet wall.

His knees buckled as another burst of gunfire pinged off the still swinging bell. Gabriella screamed, giving everything she had and forcing Harvey over the wall.

His hands found nothing to hold.

A sickening feeling rushed from his gut to his mouth as his feet left the stone floor and the empty space swallowed him whole.

The touch of stone as his hands found the parapet wall.

The jolt of his body.

One hand slipped off the smooth stone and fell away.

His boots scrambled for a foot hold, dangling from the tower.

And Gabriella rose up with raw malice in her reddened eyes, fury coursing through her veins, and her arms raised high above her head, poised to send Harvey to his death.

Through the fog of rain, a wave of angry faces burst through the gates of the marina.

The battle cry roared.

The prime minister glanced back to his family. Then, standing, he prepared to meet his fate.

"Get on the boat, sir," said Kane, grabbing his gun from the wet ground. He moved to stand before the prime minister, forcing the man behind him with his arm. Then he opened fire on the surging crowd of rebels.

The first two men dropped to the ground, their bodies trampled underfoot by the following masses, who seemed to swell with anger the closer they got.

Shoving the prime minister backward, Kane emptied his handgun into the crowd. The few that fell were swallowed by the rebels that rose over them like a wave, closing the distance.

"I said get on the damn boat, sir," said Kane to the prime minister, who was frozen to the ground with shock. "Get on the boat and get out of here."

Kane threw the gun at the storming crowd, turned, and shoved the prime minister away.

The prime minister was transfixed at the crowd of surging rebels. He walked backward with slow steps, his eyes flicking from Kane to the crowd and back at his family.

"Run, sir," shouted Kane.

He turned to face the crowd, planting his back foot into the concrete. He opened his arms and, as the first helicopter tore across the sky above the marina, the mass of rebels engulfed him, lifting him from the ground.

Blow after blow found Kane's body, rocking his head from side to side. Heavy boots connected with his back, cracking a rib that stabbed into his lung. The stamp of another foot snapped his leg back. The rounded face of a bat crushed his groin then raised into the air for a second blow.

Bright lights danced above him like angels, thundering overhead as consciousness faded in and out like the tide of the sea across broken rocks, revealing the world in all its glory then smothering it for the forces of the world to do its damage.

Black shapes fell from the bright lights.

Gunfire ripped through the night.

Kane was hoisted into the air. Vicious hands clawed at his skin and pulled at his hair as Kane approached his final battle. Death hung above him in the form of an enticing hand urging him forward.

The bat found another rib, issuing a spurt of blood from Kane's mouth. As his head fell back, his eyes fell upon the prime minister who stood leaning on the handrail of his yacht some fifty metres from the dockside.

The angry crowd hurled rocks and abuse at the boat. But those that dove into the sea were cut down by the angels from above.

For the smallest fraction of time, before the angry hands of the rebels grabbed onto his arms and legs, Kane thought he saw the prime minister offer him a smile in a shared moment of understanding. All was forgiven. The drug, Afghanistan, the murders. All of it. Every wrong decision he'd ever made.

The slate had been wiped clean.

Honour was finally his.

And as the rebels tore his body apart, the cost of his honour was death.

LITTLE WING

A BURST OF GUNFIRE RICOCHETED OFF THE BELL.

Gabriella lunged, knocking Harvey. His hands gripped the wall, but the smooth stone offered little purchase. One of his hands fell away, leaving him hanging above the street below.

She raised her arms high, summoning all of her strength. With her back arched, she let out a scream, wild and furious, as she struck to bring Harvey's knife down onto his own hand.

But Gabriella's attack was stalled mid-strike.

Three burning hot stabs of lead punched three holes into Gabriella's flesh.

The chopper maneuvered to gain a better angle.

Her attack faltered then faded away.

She dropped the knife to the stone floor.

A single shot found the flesh of her leg while two more rounds buried themselves in the stone wall.

And suddenly, everything was real.

Her father in his tan corduroys and under-vest, leaning on his garden fork, displaying the paunch with pride.

The clear profile of Francis' strong features against the

window of the car as he reached across and pulled the blanket over her.

Then the heavy boots and batons with the crack of bones and teeth and the image of her father lying in a pool of his own blood. The police moving on to find some other protester's family to destroy.

And the whomping of the helicopter overhead, shining bright lights into the car.

A gunshot.

The windscreen cracked.

More gunfire, forcing Francis off the road to Paris, where they rolled, flipped and bounced along the tarmac. Soft, wild grass had caught Gabriella in its arms when she'd been thrown from the rolling car. It left her conscious enough to see the wreckage come to a stop and Francis' body bury itself through the shattered glass.

Harvey's straining eyes stared up at her as she fell forward onto the parapet wall.

The ground below became a blur of shiny, wet cobbles in the half-light of the morning as her weight carried her over the edge.

Weightlessness as if she hovered above her memories.

A light, bright and mesmerising. She reached for it with both hands.

The ground below with its welcoming open arms.

But a strong hand found her wrist.

Her body jerked to a standstill and her feet swung in the air like lead weights that pulled her down.

She opened her eyes as a rush of wind from the chopper blades spat dust into her face, stinging like a thousand bees.

Above, Harvey looked down at her, pleading with her to hold on to his hand.

But her power was gone, her strength diminished.

The bright light worked its way across the stone wall of

the tower once more, lighting Harvey Stone like he was a fixture of the structure, a gargoyle, devoid of comedy, or anger, or fear.

Three shots sang out like the beat of a drum, the finale of a sick masterpiece. Three more rounds tore through her skin, smashing through bone and organ.

The gunman in the helicopter positioned for the final shot, signing to the pilot to turn, who was fighting the heavy wind and rain.

The time was close.

She met Harvey's eyes staring down at her from above.

He was calling to her, but the deafening beat of the helicopter swallowed all sound save for the voices of her family who called for her to join them.

Her mouth opened but the words were lost to gunfire.

Harvey screamed at the gunman.

His hand slipped further. He was hanging by the fingers of one hand with Gabriella hanging from the other.

She could feel his strength crushing her wrist.

His power was etched on his straining face.

She shook her head at Harvey Stone. The gunman fired his final shots, loosening Gabriella from Harvey's grasp as she fell into the open arms of her father.

18

STONE FREE

ACHING MUSCLES GROANED AT HARVEY'S WEIGHT AS HE hauled himself over the parapet wall then slumped to the floor, numbed by fatigue. Heavy winds forced the onslaught of rain sideways into the tower, as if it cleansed Harvey of recent events.

A momentary lull in the thundering rotor blades allowed him a reprise. Sleep crept in before reflections of the past, the present and the future could take root. Instead, the cool stone floor and patter of rain on his face allowed him to slip further into the slumber.

A hand, gentle but firm, touched his shoulder, triggering Harvey's defences.

But the darkness had him in its grip.

He lay still, open to a blade across his throat, offering himself to be cut wide open.

But no blade appeared.

The hand touched his forehead.

"We must go," said the voice of an old man, his tone urgent and hushed.

But the command faded away to thoughts of Melody, his house, and sheer silence.

Another set of hands joined the first; they gripped his shoulders and hauled Harvey to his feet.

The priest and another man, both robed and equally cautious of the circling helicopters, each took an arm to support Harvey's weight and led him to the staircase. Using the curved wall for support, Harvey descended, urged on by the priest behind, and his momentum controlled by the man in front.

The high, vaulted ceilings greeted Harvey once more, and though the daylight had been dim outside, it seemed to sing through the stained glass windows of the church.

"There's no time. They will come for you. I know a secret way out," said the priest.

He coaxed Harvey forward. The other man waited at an open door, his eyes flicking to the main entrance at the far end of the church. The priest caught the attention of his friend.

"Jacques, we will take the tunnel. Make the arrangements for Monsieur Stone's escape."

"D'accord," replied Jacques, and held the priest's gaze in a silent goodbye.

"Hold them for as long as you can," said the priest.

Nodding, Jacques walked towards the main entrance as the brakes of a car squealed to a stop outside. Voices of authority barked orders in French.

Jacques turned to face Harvey and the priest.

"Go now," he said. Then he caught Harvey's eyes. "Peace be with you."

Harvey tried to read between the lines on Jacques' face; sincerity, gratitude, fear.

Harvey replied with a nod, catching the glint in the man's eyes, then followed the priest as the church doors burst open and the sound of heavy boots echoed through the vaulted ceiling.

Lit only by the burning flame of a single torch, the two men made their way down to the very pit of the church. The staircase opened out into a larger space with arched alcoves featuring stone effigies of strong faces and bold stances that cast shadows as the flame passed by. In the ceiling, a circular opening offered a glimpse of the daylight high above. Harvey stared up at the underside of the giant bell.

"Hurry," said the priest, stopping at the entrance to a dark tunnel. "This way."

The torch flame lit the arched, stone ceiling, but faded before the end was in view.

"Can you walk?" asked the priest, securing his robes tight. "It is quite some distance."

Harvey didn't reply.

Instead, he followed the flame as heavy footsteps began to echo behind them.

They followed a series of bends, long and sweeping, as men's voices entered the tunnel. Bend after bend, the two men pushed on with their pursuers close behind. Twice, the priest stopped to help Harvey, who limped with one hand holding the wound on his leg and the other clutching his bruised ribs.

But try as he might, Harvey's broken body refused to push faster than a slow limp. They stayed one bend ahead of the men behind them until, at last, daylight lit the arched exit ahead. The priest doused the torch in a pool of rain water then broke through a tangled mass of leaves and roots. He held them high enough for Harvey to limp through after him then dropped them to cover the tunnel once more.

Shielding his eyes from the bright sunlight, Harvey followed the priest, who pulled him along with more strength than Harvey expected. The ground was soft underfoot and waves crashed close by. As Harvey's vision returned, he saw a wall of rocks to his right and the sea to his left. In the distance, the town of Saint-Pierre enjoyed the calm that follows a Mediterranean storm.

The wind had fallen. The sun had risen high. The grey sky that Harvey had stared up at from the top of the church tower had been replaced with a crisp sheet of blue, dotted with stretching fingers of white clouds that seemed to reach across the sky forcing the storm on to somewhere else.

Standing beside the rocks were two local, teenage boys, grinning from ear to ear and speaking in French too fast for Harvey to understand. They leaned on Harvey's motorcycle and beamed with pride.

"My bike," Harvey said, and turned to face the priest.

"Do not take me for a simple priest, Monsieur Stone," he said, dismissing Harvey's surprise as he walked through the soft sand. Then he gave a cautious glance back to the tunnel. "You must go. It is not safe for you. Follow the beach west and stay close to the rocks. When you are clear of the town, you will find the beach road."

Harvey pulled his injured leg over the seat. The key was in the ignition where he had left it. He pulled the clutch, turned the key, and tickled the throttle.

The engine caught on the first turn of the starter.

"Sir?" said Harvey, unsure of what to call the priest. "Thank you."

The priest appeared to relax a little. He stepped up to Harvey, placed his hand on his shoulder, and looked him in the eye with the same confidence Harvey had seen the first time they had met.

"Do not thank me, Monsieur Stone," said the priest with a smile. "France is grateful to you."

The voices in the tunnel grew louder as the men approached the exit, excited by the sight of sunlight.

"But I fear not all of France understands what you have done," said the priest.

"Is that the military or the prime minister's security?" said Harvey, gesturing to the tunnel.

"It is the police. They will be looking for somebody to charge to cover their own corruption. If they catch us, you will never see the light of day again. They are not good men."

"Will you be okay?" said Harvey.

"I will hold them," said the priest, his smile broadening. "I have God on my side. Now go, and may God be with you, Monsieur Stone."

The tangled mass of climbers and leaves burst apart and three men in police uniforms forced their way onto the beach, blinded by the sun.

With a twist of the throttle, Harvey kicked the bike into first gear, spun the back wheel, spraying sand over the men, and then tore along the beach. In his mirror, Harvey saw the men, angered and outraged at Harvey's escape, and the priest standing with the peace and confidence of a man with God by his side.

Ahead of Harvey lay a stretch of coast, long and unbroken. Bright sunlight gave the wet sand a mirror-like appearance and the glistening Mediterranean Sea offered the peace that Harvey had sought for so long. The all-terrain tyres on his motorcycle tore across the surface of the hard, wet sand, and the wind that rippled across his skin brought a new lease of life. A new direction.

He slowed to a crawl then navigated a small track that led up to the beach road where he stopped beside a small junction. A sign pointing left directed him to the village of Argeles, where Harvey would find the ruins of a once loved farmhouse, and the burned possessions of a man who owned very little.

Ahead was the French network of motorways with its

offerings of Europe, peace and solitude. London called to him with its promise of seeing Melody, Tyler, Reg and Jess. Their faces hung at the forefront of his mind.

It was Christmas Day. He imagined they would be drinking coffee by now and perhaps exchanging gifts over breakfast. He wondered if they would be thinking of him. He wondered if they understood why he sought peace.

Riding slow to savour the memories, Harvey rolled the short distance along the narrow lane to where his house once stood. The fire had consumed most of the wooden beams and only one wall still remained. The roof tiles and broken bricks were strewn across the debris, smothering any indication that the house was once somebody's home.

Pulling the bike to a stop, Harvey stepped off and began a slow walk around the perimeter of the ruin, kicking the bricks to one side and stopping on occasion. Sometimes he thought he caught a glimpse of a photo sticking out from beneath the rubble. But he knew that no photos had survived.

He stopped beside the small vegetable patch Melody had tended. The plastic sheeting had melted from the blaze to reveal six neat rows of soil like a miniature ploughed field, all devoid of life. The green leaves of the hardy, winter vegetables had singed to wafer-thin, black images of leaves, frozen in time until Harvey touched them, and they crumbled to ash.

A tiny flash of green caught Harvey's eye.

Buried under the cremated vegetables, a sole survivor stood proud. Its leaves flicked in the wind. Harvey pulled at the root, easing the carrot from its nest. It was only half-formed, but it was all that remained.

The sum total of Harvey's life in France.

He tossed the carrot onto the blackened remains of his house and thrust his hands into the pockets of his jacket.

Then he rolled his neck from side to side, waiting for the satisfying click.

But his hand found something hard and alien.

He worked his fingers into a hole in his jacket pocket he didn't know existed and fumbled until he pulled out the object.

He held the vial between finger and thumb up to the sunlight, rolling it back and forth, and staring in wonder at the red liquid.

In front of him were the ruins of his house and the remains of one dead man, one of many strewn across the town of Saint-Pierre. Harvey thought of Farrow. He thought of the guards that had died.

And all for one tiny vial of deep red liquid.

He shook his head in disbelief then let the vial fall into the palm of his hand. He rolled it back and forth, admiring the red light on his skin as the morning sun shone through the glass.

Then, taking one last look at the cause of his ruin, he dropped the vial to the ground and crushed the glass beneath his foot.

19

BOLD AS LOVE

A BLANKET OF DARK GREY CLOUD HUNG LOW IN THE SKY, so heavy it seemed as if it would crush the many couples, joggers and dog walkers beneath its weight. Standing alone on the bridge, Harvey watched the endless flow of water rush beneath him. The evening lights blinked on one by one. Their reflections in the water multiplied and fragmented.

Like broken glass.

Harvey stretched, rolling his neck from side to side and bending his legs, which were stiff from the two-day ride.

A few dots of rain found his face, inciting memories of the church tower. His hand felt his bruised ribs then lowered and touched the tender wound on his leg. In his mind, Gabriella fell from his grip.

A look of peace upon her face.

He leaned on the handrail and peered out across his city.

"I'm home," he whispered. But the sentiment failed to raise a smile.

He pushed off the railing and limped towards his bike, then hoisted his leg over and started the engine. Leaving his visor up for the cool air to rouse him for the final mile of his journey, he rolled onto the road and slipped into the light Boxing Day traffic.

At a set of lights, he came to a stop beside a bus. He could have squeezed through the gap to the front, but he had neither the energy nor the desire to lead the pack of vehicles. On the bus, sitting at the window, a man in a heavy Kashmir coat was reading a newspaper. The headline caught Harvey's eye. The traffic began to move. At the next corner shop, Harvey stopped to buy a copy and tucked it into his jacket to finish the journey.

Harvey stopped the bike in a small car park. He felt the familiar sense of relief when a long journey comes to an end and the engine shudders to a stop. Pulling the paper from his jacket, he climbed off the bike and leaned against it. The pages caught a few drops of rain that smudged the ink, but it mattered little to Harvey, who was interested in one article only.

French PM saved from assassination plot.

The sub-heading read: *La Resistance is dead*. The article described a heroic attempt to foil a plot to kill the French prime minister by a retired British army officer. There was no mention of Kane's dishonourable discharge. The reporter described the rebellion group as frustrated French citizens who were reviving the infamous French Resistance, but had only served to taint the title. The prime minister had pushed an emergency panic button to alert the French special forces, who arrived on the scene to find more than one hundred rebels attacking the PM and his family. Major Cassius Kane was killed defending the PM and forty rebels were killed in the attack.

The attack was led by Ms Gabriella DuBois, sister of Francis DuBois, the rebel leader who was killed a decade previously in a government-led attempt to eliminate rebel forces. The father of Ms DuBois was also killed less than a year ago during the angry protests that caused riots and closures of France's motorway network.

Ms DuBois was killed in the attack on the prime minister, which happened on Christmas morning. French police are looking for a man who escaped the scene and helped the Special Forces bring down Ms DuBois. The French prime minister has offered the unknown man, who wears a black leather jacket and rides a motorcycle, a reward to come forward. No other information about the vigilante is known.

Harvey closed the newspaper then rolled it up.

He pushed off his bike and limped towards the building, a small, three-story apartment block.

Flower beds lined the pathways and small areas of well-kept lawns filled the spaces between them. At the doors, Harvey was presented with a number pad to ring at the apartment. But he hadn't even raised his hand when the door burst open and Melody flung herself into his arms. He caught her and staggered back on his injured leg.

"I knew you'd come," said Melody, burying her face into his jacket and pulling herself against him, squeezing his bruised ribs. "Everyone will be so pleased to see you."

She pulled away and looked up at him, letting her eyes wander over his body. He tried to stand straight but his leg wouldn't allow it. Melody's smile faded. She said nothing but examined Harvey's posture, torn clothes and tired eyes.

She caught sight of the newspaper tucked inside Harvey's jacket.

"Did you grow bored of sitting beside the fire?" she asked, her eyebrows raised. A smile returned to her face.

Harvey shrugged.

"I hear they're looking for a man in a black leather jacket

who rides a motorcycle," said Melody, and moved in closer for another kiss.

She pulled away and raised an eyebrow once more in question, but failed to contain her grin.

Harvey didn't reply.

END OF BOOK STUFF

Stone Face - Book Twelve- Chapter One.

"One click of that button, Herman," said Luca, as he tugged at the small growth of hair he was cultivating on his chin. "That's all it takes."

Herman Hoffman held his head in his hands, squeezing his ears to stop Luca's taunting voice. The green light from the computer screen was bright in the dark room, and on the screen, monochrome cars sat in lines of traffic while pedestrians fought a perpetual battle for pavement space without breaking momentum.

"I can't," said Herman. "You can't make me do this. It is not right. It is inhuman."

But Luca raised his hand to Herman's face, stroking his skin and caressing the outside of his ear.

"I think we both know that's not true, dear Herman," replied Luca. He twisted Herman's face towards the closed door on the far side of the room. "How do you think the lovely Martina would feel about that? What do you think she will say when I tell her that her poor dear Herman has failed her and she must die?"

"Stop it," said Herman, covering his face with his fingers, and peering through the gap at the door. "Just stop it all."

"She thinks you're a failure anyway, doesn't she, Herman? Why else would she do what she did? Why else would she fall into the arms of another man?"

"You don't know that. You have no proof."

A vein, blue and thick, stuck from Luca's left temple, and his eye twitched twice, followed by the left side of his mouth.

"I have all the proof I need, Herman," said Luca. "The unexplained late nights. The missing money. And let's face it, when was the last time she kept you warm at night?"

"That's none of your business," said Herman.

"Well, I'm making it my business. If you can't be a man and stand up for yourself, perhaps I should. You're not going to let people walk all over you, are you?"

Herman stared at the door.

"No," said Herman, after a pause.

"So be a man, Herman," said Luca with a grin. "Show them who is boss."

"Does it have to be this way? Surely there must be another way."

"No," spat Luca. "It must be this way and it must be now. Strike while the iron is hot, Herman. All you have to do is hit the button on that remote, and your journey to becoming a man will begin. Albeit, a little late in life."

A tightness began to squeeze at Herman's chest.

His eyes watered, stinging from lack of sleep.

"You do want to be a man, Herman?" said Luca, running his hand through the tight curls of his dark hair, admiring his reflection in the window. "Do you want people to remember you as the man who stood up for himself? Or do you want people to remember you as the man who failed? The man who sobbed and wept and watched while his friend stood up for him and defended his honour?"

"But there are so many people down there," said Herman. "There are so many innocent people."

"Innocent?" said Luca, his mocking tone accentuating the word. "Herman, you have so much to learn. Every one of them down there is guilty of something. Every one of them deserves punishment in one form or another. And it'll be you who delivers that punishment, Herman. It's nearly time. Are you ready?"

"No," said Herman. "I can't do it."

"So then I must make a man of you myself," said Luca, still admiring his own reflection. His voice quietened. "But you must decide who is first."

Dropping his head to his hands once more, Herman pulled at his hair, letting it run between his tight knuckles. Tears fell to the carpet and a low, monotone grumble grew from the back of his throat.

"Tell me," said Luca. "I am losing my patience and the window of opportunity is closing."

"How can I decide that?"

"Shall I decide for you?" said Luca, allowing anger to slip into his tone, but then catching it and softening his words. "Who should die first? Dear little Jan?"

"No," said Herman.

But Luca continued his musings regardless of Herman's outbursts.

"He wouldn't even know it was coming. His neck would snap in my hands like a Christmas turkey, Herman."

"Stop it. How can I decide who dies? I love them both."

"Or perhaps the marvellous Martina should go first?" Luca continued. Then he stopped and stared at his reflection again in wonder at his imagination and raising a finger to his lips. "I might even have some fun with her before she goes. Now, there's a thought."

Herman raised his head from his hands. The emotion was

gone from his face, leaving nothing but anger and hatred in his eyes.

"You wouldn't," said Herman.

Luca smiled at him.

"Oh, but I would, Herman. It's not hard to imagine what she looks like beneath those slutty dresses she wears when she goes to see her fancy man, her bit on the side."

Herman's voice lowered. He stood from the desk with his back to the door and stretched his arms out to defend his wife and child from the monster that plagued his mind.

"If you lay one hand on her, Luca," he began.

"Oh, yes," said Luca, exaggerating his nonchalance.

"If you touch one hair on her body."

"There he is," said Luca, stepping forward. "That's the Herman I wanted to see."

"Get away from me," said Herman. "Leave us alone."

"All you have to do is hit the button, Herman."

Herman brought the remote up into the dim light and stared down at the single button on the rectangular device.

"That's it," said Luca, glancing at the screen and then his watch. "That's it, Herman. It is time."

But Herman studied the button as if seeing the device for the first time. He gazed past the remote and his eyes fell on the computer screen. Hundreds of people passed by in an endless flow of human activity, while the lines of cars waited for their turn to drive forward another fifty feet.

Behind Herman, the bedroom door handle squeaked as Luca began to turn it.

"I can't," said Herman, as Luca pushed the door open to reveal Martina tied to the bed, her eyes wide and pleading. But the gag in her mouth prevented any sound other than a high-pitched muffle to escape. Jan was sitting on the floor, his hands bound to the bed frame and a hood pulled over his face.

"So then I'll decide," said Luca. His voice had dropped to a whisper. He stepped across the threadbare carpet to where Martina began to thrash against her restraints. Turning to face the bedroom window, he let a serious look of hatred wipe away his expression of delight.

"Stop it," said Herman, pleading with Luca to end the torment.

"The button," said Luca.

The muscles in Herman's body slumped. His shoulders sagged and his voice quietened in an effort to reason with the man.

"There are hundreds of people down there," said Herman. "Who do you think you are?"

"Push the button, Herman," said Luca, as he flicked at Martina's hair with his index finger then traced the outline of her face to her chest.

"No," said Herman. "Just stop it. Let them go."

But Luca's wandering hands were already unbuttoning Martina's dress.

"Tick tock, Herman."

"Okay, okay."

Hearing the change in Herman's voice, Luca looked up. His groping hand paused.

Martina stared at her husband. A look of dread filled her eyes.

"I'll do it," said Herman, holding the remote in the air.

Luca smiled.

"So you've decided to become a man, my dear Herman."

With his eyes locked onto his wife's in a look of apology and despair, Herman pushed the button.

A NOTE FROM THE AUTHOR

Stone Army was one of the hardest, but most enjoyable of the Stone Cold Thriller series to write.

I felt Harvey needed some time alone to enjoy the life he'd worked so hard for; that peace and solitude he seeks.

And then I thought I'd shake things up a little. London is where he belongs. London is where his heart is.

And London needs him.

I hope you'll stick around for his next set of adventures. It is my aim to take you by surprise. It is my hope to make you gasp as you turn each page. And it is my pleasure to take you away into Harvey's world to share in his adventures.

Thank you for reading.

J.D. Weston

To learn more about J.D. Weston

www.jdweston.com
john@jdweston.com

ALSO BY J.D.WESTON.

The Stone Cold Thriller Series.

Book 1 - Stone Cold

Book 2 - Stone Fury

Book 3 - Stone Fall

Book 4 - Stone Rage

Book 5 - Stone Free

Book 6 - Stone Rush

Book 7 - Stone Game

Book 8 - Stone Raid

Book 9 - Stone Deep

Book 10 - Stone Fist

Book 11 - Stone Army

Book 12 - Stone Face

Novellas

Stone Breed

Stone Blood

The Alaskan Adventure

Where the Mountains Kiss the Sun

From the Ocean to the Stream

.

STONE COLD

Book One of the Stone Cold Thriller series

One priceless set of diamonds. Three of London's ruthless east end crime families. One very angry assassin with a hit list.

Harvey Stone has questions that someone will answer. Who killed his parents and why? Who raped and killed his sister? And why are his closest allies hiding the truth.

When Harvey is asked to kill east London's biggest crime boss in return for one name on his list, there is only one answer.

Can Harvey survive the gang war, untangle the web of deceit and uncover the truth behind his sisters death?

Stone Cold is the first book in the Stone Cold thriller series.

If you enjoy fast-paced adventure, gritty vigilante stories and no-nonsense heroes, then you'll love J.D. Weston's brand new Thriller Series.

STONE FURY

Book Two of the Stone Cold Thriller series

The lives of twelve young girls are being sold. The seller is on Harvey Stone's hit list.

When ex-hitman Harvey Stone learns of an human trafficking ring taking place in his old stomping ground, he is sickened. But when he learns the name of the person running the show, an opportunity arises to cross one more name of his list.

Can Harvey save the ill-fated girls, and serve justice to those who are most deserved?

Stone Fury is the second book in the Stone Cold thriller series.

If you enjoy fast-paced adventure, gritty vigilante stories and no-nonsense heroes, then you'll love J.D. Weston's brand new Thriller Series.

STONE FALL

Book Three of the Stone Cold Thriller series

One evil terrorist with a plan to change the face of London. One missing child, and one priceless jade Buddha. Only Harvey Stone and his team of organised crime specialists can prevent disaster.

When Harvey and the team intercept a heist to rob a priceless jade Buddha, little did they know they would be uncovering a terrorist attack on London's St Paul's Cathedral, and a shocking hostage scenario.

Can Harvey and the team stop the terrorists, save the little girl and rescue the priceless Buddha?

Stone Fall is the third book in the Stone Cold thriller series.

If you enjoy fast-paced adventure, gritty vigilante stories and no-nonsense heroes, then you'll love J.D. Weston's brand new Thriller Series.

STONE RAGE

Book Four of the Stone Cold Thriller series

Two of east London's most notorious gangs go head to head with the Albanian mafia, and one angry assassin who's out to clean up.

When Harvey Stone is sent undercover to put a stop a turf war between the Albanian mafia and two of East London's most notorious gangs, nobody expected him to be welcomed like a hero by an old face.

Has Harvey finally gone rogue, or will he put a stop to the bloodshed once and for all?

Stone Rage is the fourth book in the Stone Cold thriller series.

If you enjoy fast-paced adventure, gritty vigilante stories and no-nonsense heroes, then you'll love J.D. Weston's brand new Thriller Series.

STONE FREE

Book Five of the Stone Cold Thriller series

Death by internet. A mind blowing masterplan, where death holds all the cards.

Harvey Stone plays guardian angel on international soil when two governments prepare to do battle, and the lives of innocent people are at stake.

Can Harvey free the condemned women and avert an international disaster. Can he defy all odds and escape alive?

Find out in Stone Free, the fifth book in the Stone Cold Thriller series.

If you enjoy intense thrillers, with shocking storylines, then you'll love this new series from J.D. Weston.

STONE RUSH

Book Six of the Stone Cold Thriller series

Europe's slave trade is alive. MI6 is falling down, and Harvey Stone is caught in the middle.

Harvey yearns for the quiet life, but when a close friend is captured and tortured, and refugees become slaves, Harvey is forced out of retirement.

Can Harvey put a stop to the human traffickers and save the girls from a torturous death? Can he prevent the gang's devastating plans?

Find out, in Stone Rush, the sixth book in the Stone Cold Thriller series.

If you enjoy intense thrillers, with shocking storylines, then you'll love this new action crime thriller from J.D. Weston.

STONE GAME

Book Seven of the Stone Cold Thriller series

Tragedy strikes. A killer runs wild, and an old enemy raises the stakes.

Memories of Harvey's kills return to haunt his freedom. But as the body count grows and the past become reality, the hunter becomes the hunted.

Has Harvey gone back to his old ways? Is he destined for a life on the run?

Stone Game is the seventh book in J.D. Weston's Stone Cold Thriller series.

If you like your action hard and fast, with page-turning intensity, you'll love this series.

STONE RAID

Book Eight of the Stone Cold Thriller series

A pair of cursed diamonds. A brutal gang ran by evil twin brothers. And an ex-hitman who finds himself deep inside a Victorian legend.

When ex-hitman Harvey Stone emerges from laying low, he stumbles into a cruel and twisted plot devised by evil twin brothers to bring together two cursed diamonds, and unleash hell in London.

But the deeper Harvey delves into their plans, the more twisted they become, and saving the diamonds becomes his toughest challenge yet.

Can Harvey bring down the evil twins and prevent the cursed diamonds from destroying more lives? Can he find right from wrong in this twisted tale of lies and deceit?

STONE DEEP

Book Nine of the Stone Cold Thriller series

An ancient Spanish legacy. A shocking explosion in the City of London. And an ex-hitman fueled by revenge.

When ex-hitman, Harvey Stone is asked by an art collector, Smokey the Jew, to kidnap a member of a rival gang and extract details of a heist, little did he know the move would open the doors of hell and endanger everyone he cares for.

But renowned art thief, Dante Dumas will go to any length to find his family legacy, killing anyone who stands in his way.

Can Harvey survive Dante's devious plans, and can he find retribution for his lost love?

STONE FIST

Book Ten of the Stone Cold Thriller series

Two East London gangs. One ex-hitman clinging to the past. And a brutal fight to the death.

When ex-hitman Harvey Stone visits London to attend the wedding of one of his closest allies, he plans a visit to the grave of his long-dead mentor, Julios. But little does Harvey know that the trip will uncover a secret that will change his life forever and open doors to Harvey's past that have never before been revealed. But to forge an allegiance with a blast from Harvey's past he must first deal with a brutal death match between two rival gangs that threatens to wipe history from the face of the earth before it's even exposed.

STONE ARMY

Book Eleven of the Stone Cold Thriller series

A twisted assassination plot. A deadly super-drug is born. And Harvey Stone is hell-bent on revenge.

Harvey Stone seeks peace and solitude, choosing to spend Christmas alone in his farmhouse in southern France, when four armed men leap from a helicopter to question him about a missing girl.

But when a leading scientist is found dead and the missing girl arrives on Harvey's doorstep, a sequence of events unfolds that push the boundaries of human performance to its deadly limits.

ACKNOWLEDGMENTS

Authors are often portrayed as having very lonely work lives. There breeds a stereotypical image of reclusive authors talking only to their cat or dog and their editor, and living off cereal and brandy.

I beg to differ.

There is absolutely no way on the planet that this book could have been created to the standard it is without the help and support of Erica Bawden, Paul Weston, Danny Maguire, and Heather Draper. All of whom offered vital feedback during various drafts and supported me while I locked myself away and spoke to my imaginary dog, ate cereal and drank brandy.

The book was painstakingly edited by Ceri Savage, who continues to sit with me on Skype every week as we flesh out the series, and also threw in some amazing ideas.

To those named above, I am truly grateful.

J.D. Weston.

Printed in Germany
by Amazon Distribution
GmbH, Leipzig